IRRESISTIBLE

SECOND EDITION

BOOK ONE

THE BLOODLUST CHRONICLES

TARA VASSER

Copyright© Winter Musings LLC **2019**

978-1-947882-26-3 PRINT

978-1-947882-27-0 MOBI

978-1-947882-28-7 EPUB

978-1-947882-29-4 AUDIOBOOK

Editing By: Leanore Elliot

Cover Art By: DuskTilDawn Designs

Photo Credit:

Royal Touch Photography

IRRESISTIBLE

2ND EDITION

IRRESISTIBLE, SECOND EDITION IS BOOK ONE
OF THE BLOODLUST CHRONICLES.

DEDICATION

To The Viking – Thanks for patiently listening to me
whine about how difficult this rewrite was. I couldn't
ask for a better partner!

ACKNOWLEDGEMENTS

Special thanks go out to:

Ashley for all your feedback and encouragement, without you, I would still be rewriting this.

Michel and Jennell for being the best critique partners I could ask for. You're amazing, thanks for helping me make this a better story.

Royal Touch Photography for the amazing photos.

Mandy and Chase for taking hot pictures to put on book covers.

Dusk Til Dawn Designs for creating a new cover!

Leanore for reminding me a good editor makes the story a bazillion times better (yes, I used the word bazillion).

Elisabeth Naughton. Marked was the first romance novel that I fell in love with and escaped from postpartum depression into. Theron literally saved my sanity. Your story of becoming an author was my inspiration for writing a book of my own.

You! The amazing readers! Without you, there is no story. I hope you enjoy what's in store for you with the second edition of *Irresistible*.

Foreword

First off, I just want to thank you for taking a chance on the second edition of *Irresistible* and giving it a read. In case you are unaware, this is a re-written edition of *Irresistible*, book one of *The Bloodlust Chronicles*, published in 2016. For those of you who read the first edition, you will find quite a few differences in the interactions between our main characters.

There are a few things you should know about the first edition that might explain why it turned out the way it did. The first is that it wasn't meant to be more than one book. Irresistible was written in the middle of many nights as a way to combat post-partum depression. Writing was the only thing keeping me relatively sane. It gave me a world to disappear into when mine felt pretty awful. When I decided to publish *Irresistible*, I wanted to put it out there purely to check publishing a book off my bucket list.

The second thing to know is that the first edition of *Irresistible* wasn't written as a romance novel. I ended up deciding to change the story to make it more marketable as a romance, because the central focus was the relationship between Nora and Endre. This leads me to the third thing to know; in the very first drafts of Irresistible, this single, stand-alone story, ended *very* differently. It wasn't a happily ever after, or a happily for now. That first ending made sense with the extreme violence between Nora and Endre. When I changed the end, I didn't change the rest of the story. I should have, but I didn't.

That disparity between the end and the rest of the story is answer to why I decided to rewrite. The story you read didn't fit with the ending I gave it. Although the reviews were generally accepting of *Irresistible* as a decent dark paranormal romance, that's not what it was supposed to be and there were reviewers who let me know that. I received reviews from readers commenting that the relationship between Nora and Endre portrayed in the first edition was abusive, all because of the new ending. At the time of publication, I didn't see the relationship like that, because this was my book. My baby. My blood, sweat, and tears went into this book. Since re-reading, I get it. So I've changed the dynamic between Nora and Endre.

However, I will state that this second edition does contain blood and violence. We *are* talking about Vampires here! I hope you enjoy this second edition of Irresistible.

If you have not read the first edition of Irresistible, and are curious enough to want to read it, you can find it here on BookFunnel for free:

https://dl.bookfunnel.com/i31ucokua7

IRRESISTIBLE

SECOND EDITION

Buried as punishment for a crime he didn't commit, Endre has had nothing but time to plot revenge on his betrayer. Salvation arrives when an archaeology student unwittingly exhumes his coffin and provides him with the first blood he's tasted in nearly a century.

Upon awakening from an attack by a creature she never believed existed, Nora discovers she is now his hostage. Forced to accompany Endre from Italy to Paris on a quest for vengeance, she is thrust into his dark and forbidden world and finds herself inexplicably drawn to the Vampire. Lust runs rampant throughout the course of their journey and Nora begins to question if the irresistible connection between them is more than mere biology.

PROLOGUE

1923 – Italy

Endre sat beneath the shadow of a massive cork tree in his garden, reading the newspaper as he watched the first rays of sunshine peek over the hills to the east. It was a pity he could not give his full attention to the beautiful view, his mind burdened with the troubling headlines. Folding the paper with a deep sigh, he pushed the paper and his thoughts of Mussolini's latest moves to overtake parliament to the side. Perhaps it was time to leave Italy and move on to greener pastures. There was an ominous scent in the wind, and it spoke of the death and destruction on the horizon.

Endre was no stranger to war and chaos, having been born a warrior. When conflicts arose in the world around him, his hands always itched to take up sword and shield. But of course, those days of ending wars with steel were over. Now, the weapons of choice were guns and bombs. There was no honor in that. No promises of glory or feasting in the halls of Valhalla when so little skill and preparation was involved.

Valhalla or no, the political climate of this region was no longer hospitable to his research. Secrecy was completely necessary, and the alliances Gregor had forged to provide Endre with supplies for his lab would not stand the threat this new breed of fascism posed. Glancing over at the horizon, he frowned. He had been out here long enough; it was time to retire for the day, and he would allow his dreams to conjure his next moves and put new plans into place when twilight fell. Endre picked up his paper and made his way toward the door when the noise of automobile tires crunching over the gravel drive and shouting stilled his movement.

"Back here! In the garden!" a voice hollered from the garden entrance.

A man dressed impeccably in a suit with a homburg gracing his head stood at the entrance of the sanctuary. Endre did not recall his name, he only knew the man as one of Lorenzo's bodyguards. The man gestured wildly in Endre's direction.

Several more of Lorenzo's bodyguards filed in behind him, posturing menacingly.

Confused, Endre watched the men as they lined the perimeter of his garden, violating his last few moments before the sun crested over the hill. "What is this? Where is Lorenzo?" he scoffed, standing his ground when they surrounded him where he stood, preparing to fight if the need arose.

"I am here," Lorenzo's French-accented voice called leisurely from the garden entrance as he strolled forward and casually buttoned his suit jacket.

Sighing with relief, Endre relaxed at the sight of his friend.

Lorenzo sauntered into the garden lazily, stopping to inspect a blossom before meandering his way through his men to stand in front of Endre.

"And to what do I owe this honor?" Endre questioned suspiciously, watching Lorenzo carefully. It was much too close to dawn for them to be conducting business.

"Endre, you have been charged with murder," Lorenzo recited in a bored voice, placing his hands in his pockets and rocking back on his heels.

Endre's head jerked back as if he had been struck. Murder? He was being charged with murder? "And who is it exactly that I am supposed to have killed?" Endre demanded, outrage making his voice boom through the still morning air.

"Count La Rossa." Lorenzo sighed sadly. "Why did you do it, Endre?"

"You cannot be serious." Endre balked, sure this was some prank. "Gregor is dead?"

The men surrounding him took a step closer, as if of one mind.

"I did not kill Gregor," Endre protested, though he found himself falling back on his training from another life and crouched into a fighting stance.

Several more men joined the mob, men from Gregor's guard, flanking Endre now with more than a dozen men. At most, he could take out half of them before they would bring him down, leaving another half dozen to beat him mercilessly and likely kill him in the process—merely for resisting. Any defiance would be futile, but he would not go down without a fight, especially for a false charge.

Lorenzo shook his head sadly at Endre's change in demeanor, as if his instincts of self-preservation condemned him of the crimes for which he was accused. Lorenzo raised his voice loud so all the men could hear him. "Endre, you are hereby charged with the murder of Count Gregor La Rossa. Your brothers here will serve as judge, jury, and executioners of your sentence. The traditional punishment for such a crime, as you are well aware, is burial. Your death by starvation will serve as justice by the old laws laid forth by The Council. Guards, seize him and prepare him for his punishment." Then, turning back to Endre, he taunted, "I think we will bury you here in your beloved garden."

Several of the guards pulled out pistols and made moves toward Endre.

Cowards, of course, they would not face him without firearms.

Endre lashed out, but he had only his fists. He managed to knock two of the guards to the ground before they had him pinned to the moldering leaves in the dirt.

Fists were no match for bullets.

Watching with one eye—the other caked in blood and dirt—three men began digging his grave beneath the large tree and another two hauled a plain coffin through the garden gates.

At the sight of the coffin, Endre redoubled his struggled to break free. "Lorenzo, this is nonsense. Gregor was my oldest friend and confidant. He was like a brother to me, just as you are. I would never harm him. What is the evidence against me? I demand a trial with The Council. It is my right," he spoke around the dirt in his mouth.

Scowling down at him disapprovingly, Lorenzo approached slowly. He stooped and picked up Endre's fallen fedora, brushing dirt from the fabric.

An entreating glance at Lorenzo earned Endre naught but a kick to the face. This man was no friend. Endre wondered if he had ever been. Blood from a gash above his eye poured down his face, but healed almost as quickly as it occurred, leaving dried blood caked to his eyelashes. Through crusted lashes, he watched as Lorenzo stood above him and removed his own hat, placing Endre's atop his head instead.

Smiling, Lorenzo gave a nod of approval at Endre's taste in men's fashion and tossed his hat to one of the men standing guard, inciting a round of chuckles from his henchmen.

Fury boiled in Endre's veins as his 'friend' betrayed him and made light of the unlawful punishment he dealt. How could Lorenzo believe Endre capable of such a crime? It was unlike Lorenzo to dole out consequence without following proper protocol.

Unless Lorenzo had something to hide. Something he worried The Council would unearth if the matter were brought to trial.

Realization sunk like a stone in Endre's gut as he put the pieces together.

When the guards finished digging the grave, the men casually tossed the coffin into the pit at Lorenzo's gesture. The dull thud sent a chill through Endre. He continued to struggle against his captors, but with three of them now detaining him, he received nothing but a pistol whip to the head and kicks to his ribs.

With a nod from Lorenzo, the guards hauled Endre to his feet and dragged him toward the yawning opening of the coffin awaiting him. At the foot of the open box, two of the guards held his arms while one bound his hands in front of him with thick rope. Endre let out a shout when one man grabbed his hair and held his head back so he gazed directly into the lightening sky. From the corner of his eye, Endre watched Lorenzo pull a wicked-looking dagger from a sheath at his hip. The blade glinted with the light of the rising sun, a shining omen of Endre's imminent demise.

"Lorenzo, please," Endre spoke to the man before him, the man he had considered a friend until this day, "I—"

Lorenzo only gave Endre a devious grin and prevented any more words from escaping his lips with a quick slash of his blade across Endre's neck. Blood cascaded from his neck and he choked as it drained into his throat. Within seconds, the wound had already begun to heal itself, the blood flow stanched. Lorenzo's blade dashed out again, performing the same motion across the nearly-healed laceration. Again, Endre choked and sputtered on his own warm blood and any words he wished to speak.

Light-headed from the blood loss, Endre fell to his knees. The guards holding him stepped back and left him with Lorenzo glowering down at him. Endre's head lolled to the side and he was barely clinging to consciousness. All it took was a well-placed kick from Lorenzo and he fell backward into his new prison.

Several of the guards made a move to place the lid on the coffin, but Lorenzo stayed their movement with a wave of his hand. "Leave us. I want to speak to this murderous traitor alone before we leave him to the worms," Lorenzo ordered, his eyes never leaving Endre's fading ones.

Several murmurs went through the small crowd. That was not the way. Tradition and adherence to the old laws stated the sentence must be carried out before an amassing of the people, so all could witness what fate befell a murderer of his own kind.

"Leave us!" Lorenzo roared, turning to stare down each man in turn.

The guards filed from the garden, leaving Endre with Lorenzo and his bloody blade.

Lorenzo couched so his face was close to Endre's.

Endre only wished enough blood had still flowed in his veins so he could reach out and relieve Lorenzo of the triumphant smile gracing his lips.

"Endre," Lorenzo whispered with a sigh, "I warned you not to approach Gregor to back your research, and yet you did. Not only that, expressing wishes to distribute your cure at no cost?" Lorenzo tsked and shook his head. "He would have done it, too. Threatened to expose me for lack of loyalty to our people. Unfortunately, he miscalculated. The man was too much of a philanthropist for his own good. He never did understand the power his money held. Such a waste. And here we are. Someone has to take the fall for Gregor's death and *justice* must be served. It might as well be you. His blood is on your hands as much as mine, all because you could not follow simple directions. We could have profited from this together, you and I. I would kill you now if it would not upset the delicate sensibilities of our people. But alas, I cannot. Perhaps in a century or two, I will come check on you and finish the task when everyone has forgotten your existence."

Endre glared up at Lorenzo, the lack of blood preventing his wounds from healing and allowing him to foil his new enemy's plans.

"But do not worry," Lorenzo continued, brushing dirt from his trousers. "I will not let your research go to waste. I still have plans for the work you have done, but perhaps an adjustment here and there to suit my own needs."

Endre only had the faintest inkling of what kind of dastardly plans Lorenzo was concocting, but the malicious smile gracing his lips was indication enough that it would not be good.

Rising to his feet, Lorenzo glanced down impassively at Endre once more. "You should have listened to me, old friend. Now, you will have plenty of time to think on your cure and the error of your ways while you rot in your grave," Lorenzo spat out with a maniacal laugh. Bending over, he slashed out with his blade one last time.

Endre felt the slightest trickle of blood ooze from the cut, so little of the liquid remained in his body.

At a shouted order from Lorenzo, the guards all marched back into the garden.

Endre attempted to alert them to Lorenzo's treachery, but the only sound from his mangled throat was a pained moan. The lid of the coffin was lowered, blocking out the dazzling sunshine of the new morning, and hammers pounded out the finality of his death sentence. The last glimpse Endre had of Lorenzo was a mocking tip of the hat, *his* hat.

This box would not hold Endre forever, and when he rose, he intended to rain down retribution, and when he came for Lorenzo, it would be all-out war. The last thing he could hear between his own thoughts of revenge and each shovelful of dirt falling on the wooden box was Lorenzo whistling happily with the belief he had gotten away with his crimes.

CHAPTER ONE

Present Day

"Alright, class, that's it for today's lecture," Professor Hoffman concluded before turning back to face his students. "However," he shouted above the suddenly deafening noise of books shoved into backpacks and students rushing to get to their next classes, "I do have a few announcements."

The entire class groaned in unison and the din died down to a rustle of papers and the occasional zipper.

Nora's attention snapped from the bluebird hopping from branch to branch in the enormous oak tree outside the lecture hall's window to Professor Hoffman at the front of the room. It wasn't like her to allow her thoughts to drift so much during class. In fact, she usually loved this course. Lately, though, she was finding it difficult to concentrate through the haze of exhaustion. Even her roommate Chloe had noticed her dragging, forcing Nora to make an appointment with the campus clinic.

"There is a dig opportunity in Italy that has just come up," the professor hinted, pausing for the class's rapt attention, which he quickly received.

It was as if a switch had been flicked and all the air was sucked from the room. The silence was stifling. Every student held their breath, waiting for the rest of the announcement. Even Nora's attention was single-mindedly focused on the professor.

Most days, she just wanted to blend into the crowd, avoiding eye contact, lest she get called on to answer questions. She didn't like being singled out in class discussions to point out that she knew the answers. She'd told herself during her senior year of high school that college would change her label as nerd or a geek. She would have adventures, friends and fun. Nora had planned to dress up in sexy little dresses and attend wild parties where she would drink too much and dance with wild abandon. But here she was still the responsible, studious one, four years later. This announcement could make the lack of fun and wild abandon all worthwhile; it could be just what she needed to make that hard work pay off and jumpstart a career for when she graduated.

"Since this is a prime opportunity for a select few of you to gain some field experience, I am restricting the applications to seniors only," the professor said, his voice booming through the lecture hall amidst the groans of the underclassmen, whose attention evaporated into the ether. "If you are a senior, and you have a B plus or above, I welcome your applications. I have them up here," he enticed, thumbing the edge of the papers as though he was counting a small fortune. "Come to the front of the room with questions. Class is dismissed."

Her exhaustion all but absent, Nora rushed to the front of the room. The dig was a once in a lifetime opportunity she *had* to know more about.

"Nora!" Professor Hoffman exclaimed with a smile as she approached his desk. "Are you applying for the dig?"

"I was still debating, actually," Nora wavered, biting her lip and forcing her gaze upward from her shoes to meet his eyes.

"There's nothing to debate. You've got the top grade in the class. I will guarantee one of the three spots is yours if you want to go," he affirmed, leaning back against the desk and crossing his arms, an expression akin to disapproval settling on his face.

Nora's eyes grew wide as her brain attempted to process what he had just said. He was *guaranteeing* her a spot? Disbelief and a little bit of terror stole all other thoughts from her brain.

"Think about it, but not too long," he warned, handing Nora a sheet of paper before returning to the other side of the desk to retrieve his laptop bag.

Nora hardly noticed him leave as she stared at the paper gripped in her shaking hands. Dropping her backpack to the floor, she sank into the seat of the nearest desk, worried her shaking legs would fail her.

This was it. This was her big adventure.

Fate had brought this opportunity to her; it would be bad manners to fling it back in her face, wouldn't it? Quickly pulling a pen from her backpack, Nora filled out the form, trying to ignore the tremors making her writing nearly illegible. Once every space was filled in, she threw her pen back into her bag and pulled her bag onto her back with renewed vigor. Running down the hall to Professor Hoffman's office, she was determined to put the form into his hands before she lost her nerve, barely catching him before he locked his door.

"Here," she panted, thrusting the paper at him. "I'm in. I want to go," she announced, pushing her glasses up the bridge of her nose.

Professor Hoffman broke into a huge grin. He took the paper from her and shook her sweaty, shaking hand. "Welcome aboard, Nora!" he exclaimed excitedly. "Come here on Wednesday around noon for a meeting to go through the particulars."

Nora nodded mutely as Professor Hoffman brushed past her and left her standing in the hall outside his office, paralyzed with disbelief. She was going to Italy on her first real archeological dig. Suppressing an uncharacteristic excited squeal which threatened to escape from her, she sprinted the whole way back to her dorm, thoughts of exhaustion and blood tests completely forgotten.

In less than two weeks, Nora would be in a different country on a different continent. It was all exciting, overwhelming, and absolutely terrifying.

CHAPTER TWO

Over the next several days leading up to departure for the trip, Nora alternately attempted to pack everything she could possibly need for an international trip and tried desperately not to throw up. In her head, she made big plans to travel across Italy and see the sights in Rome, Florence, Venice, and wherever her dreams took her. Lying on her stomach with her feet kicked up in the air like a teenage girl looking through a gossip magazine, she pored over the Italy travel guide she'd picked up from the campus bookstore.

"Firenze. Venezia," Nora whispered to herself, trying out the foreign words on her tongue. Memorizing every detail of the pictures and attempting to wrap her brain around the Italian pronunciations, she worked on narrowing down her wish list of tourist traps.

"Are you still reading that thing?" Chloe, her best friend and roommate, inquired with a laugh. "Are you actually going to see all those places you've marked with your little tabs?" She gestured to the fluorescent pink slips of paper protruding from the guidebook.

"I want to! I just don't know if I'll be able to." Nora groaned, burying her face in her pillow.

"Why not?" Chloe pressed, sitting next to her on the bed and taking the book. Flipping through the pages, she stopped to admire several pictures of the Ponte Vecchio in Florence Nora had tagged. "Will you be working the entire time, or do you get weekends off to go see these things?" she asked, waving the book at her roommate.

"It's not time I'm worried about. I just don't know if I can do it, you know?" Nora whined, rolling onto her side and reaching for the book.

"No, I don't know, Nora," Chloe countered, narrowing her eyes and holding the book out of Nora's grasp. "You get this incredible opportunity to travel to Italy. Freaking *Italy*, Nora. You damn well better go and see all this stuff, this is all you've ever wanted to do with your life. I know it's not Norway, or whatever your dream destination is, but Italy has some amazing rich history and mythology."

It was true. She'd always known she wanted to study lives and stories of the past. The influence of her grandmother's elaborate tales of Norse mythology were to blame for Nora's single-minded determination to study archaeology.

Nodding, Nora reached for the book again. "We're going to this estate in Tuscany, just outside of Siena. It's owned by a guy Professor Hoffman knows, Mr. Micelli. I guess he's refurbishing this big villa to make it into a fancy spa. The construction crew was digging to repair the foundation and they found something he thinks might be an ancient Roman artifact."

"Why fly people all the way from the U.S. instead of using students from Italy?" Chloe questioned, frowning at a page in the book.

"I don't know, I suppose because he knows and trusts Professor Hoffman? Really, I'm not sure. Something about checking into it before the government seizes it." Nora shrugged. All the information came at her so fast when the professor was explaining everything to her and the other two attending students, she hadn't really had much time to absorb it all.

"That sounds fishy. I mean, it's probably on the up and up, but it's kind of weird," Chloe said as she furrowed her brow when meeting Nora's gaze.

"I don't think Professor Hoffman would get us into something illegal. At least not intentionally," Nora defended. She'd had Professor Hoffman for a few different classes now, and he did not strike her as the type to get involved with illegal activities. Nora reached for the book again, worried all Chloe's paging would dislodge her carefully placed tags.

"Who else is going?" Chloe held the book away from Nora's grabbing hands while she flipped to each bright pink page marker.

"Two other people from my class, Tom and Judy, I think their names are." Nora wracked her brain for confirmation on the names. She wasn't the most social of people, preferring books to human interaction most times, so the names of her classmates didn't usually stick with her.

"Is he cute?"

"Who?"

"Professor Hoffman," Chloe said with a guffaw, then rolled her eyes. "The Tom guy from your class."

"I don't know, kinda, I guess so."

"What about the Italian guy?" Chloe peeked up over the edge of the book with a smirk.

"I haven't seen him, so I don't know." Nora shrugged.

"But he's Italian, and has enough money to buy property in Italy. That might make him cute enough."

Wiggling her eyebrows suggestively, Chloe fanned herself with the open book.

Nora snorted when she laughed. "I'm sure he's some old guy if he's friends with Professor Hoffman."

"That's a shame." Chloe frowned. "You really need a guy."

"I do not want a guy," Nora protested, rising from the bed and grabbing at the shirts piled atop her dresser.

"I didn't say *want*. I said *need*. They have the necessary equipment to help you with your v-card problem."

"You say that like having my virginity is an affliction." Nora glowered at her best friend while she threw shirts into the open suitcase at the end of the bed.

Chloe shrugged. "Maybe a hot Italian guy can convince you to give it up." When her gaze met Nora's she rolled her eyes. "Of course, that won't happen. Not if I'm not there to be your wingwoman. Girl, you *have* to loosen up and have fun while you're on this trip." Waving the book, she stood. "In fact, I want to see pictures of you at all these places, and *especially* on the back of some hot Italian guy's motorcycle." Biting her lip, she glanced to the ceiling. "I think I saw that in a movie once."

"I'm sure I'll be working too much to pick up guys," Nora said, stifling a yawn.

Chloe's expression morphed from playful to concerned. "Did you see that doctor today?"

Nora nodded, covering another yawn.

"And she said you could travel?" A furrow formed between Chloe's brows as she eyed Nora suspiciously.

"She didn't say I *couldn't*," Nora hedged with a shrug.

"Did you even ask her?"

"No," Nora admitted reluctantly as she scratched at the tape holding a cotton ball to the little red dot from the needle stick. "This is ridiculous, you know. People go to the doctor when they're sick, not tired. I just need more sleep. I mean, of *course* I'm tired. I'm taking a full course load."

"Nora, you sleep more than I do, and that's saying something. Is that what she said, that you just need more sleep?"

"You worry too much." Nora turned back to the clothes she dug from her drawers and tossed them haphazardly into the suitcase. She'd organize them later when she figured out exactly what she was bringing and how much she could fit.

"What did she say?"

With a sigh, Nora met her best friend's penetrating gaze. "Nothing. She took some blood to run some tests and said she'd get back to me with the results."

"So, she doesn't have any ideas? When do you get the results back?"

"She said it might be mono. There were some other things she wanted to look into, too."

"When do you find out?"

"The lady in the lab said it could take up to two weeks. Can we be done with the interrogation? You're worse than my mom." Nora sighed and turned back to her open dresser drawer.

"*Two weeks*?" Chloe scoffed. "You won't even find out before you leave. What if you have mono? What if it's something worse? You'll be on an entirely different continent."

"Then I'll go to a doctor there. I can't *not* go to the dig because something *might* be wrong. Can we please not talk about this right now?" Nora pleaded with exasperation.

Chloe pursed her lips and tossed the guidebook at Nora. "Fine, no more talk about doctors. What clothes are you bringing?" she demanded as she moved toward Nora's open suitcase between their beds. "Please tell me you aren't bringing those god-awful cargo pants you wear all the time," she pleaded, pawing through the stacks of clothing. "At least bring a cute dress to go to a fancy dinner or something... Wait, what is this, Nora?" Chloe held up a tattered, black Metallica shirt pinched between her thumb and forefinger like it was some vile creature.

"Oh, it's nothing." Nora reached for the shirt, warmth rushing to her cheeks.

Chloe sighed at her. "Well, that's funny, because I seem to remember some sleazy asshole wearing this nasty thing all the time," Chloe challenged, wrinkling her nose at the shirt and looking over at Nora. "Honey, it's time to let that jackass go. As soon as John realized you weren't putting out, he moved on, it's time you do, too," she chided, holding the shirt out of Nora's reach and sitting on the bed again.

Nora nodded, fighting the stinging of oncoming tears that prickled behind her eyes.

"I know you liked him, but he wasn't who you thought he was."

"I know," Nora whispered with a sigh, thinking back to the way he'd morphed from patient and understanding about her desire to go slow with the physical aspects of their relationship, to relentless in his pursuit of sex. Maybe if she hadn't been so scared and just gave it up to him, he would have been different.

"I see that look on your face. Don't you dare think for one second that you did anything wrong. You are amazing and wonderful, and he was not worthy of you," Chloe consoled, her brows pinched together in concern.

"You're right," Nora croaked out around the frog in her throat. "I just wish I could have done things differently."

"I don't think you're hearing me. He. Him. You could have fucked him every day, and he *still* would have been an asshole."

Nora wasn't so sure that was true. He'd practically been prince charming when they'd met and then one day, everything just changed.

"Okay, I can see I'm not getting through to you, so let me refresh your memory with some harsh realities. Nora, he left you in the parking lot at a concert in the middle of nowhere because you wouldn't give him a blowjob. Do you remember that? Because I do— having been the one to drive for *hours* in the pouring rain to pick you up. I spent more time dealing with the fallout from your relationship than I spent with you," Chloe practically screamed at her. "Stop trying to blame this on yourself. Stop trying to make excuses for him."

Hanging her head, Nora bit her lip and attempted to stave off her threatening tears.

Chloe, undeterred by Nora's emotional distress, continued on her tirade, "I'm sorry to be so harsh, but that's what best friends are for, to give you the big fat reality check and the slap upside the head you need. This isn't some unrequited love where you should keep his nasty shirt to remember him," Chloe reprimanded, wrapping her arms around Nora.

"I know, I'm totally pathetic," Nora said with a sniff. "He was just so sweet in the beginning, I always thought I could get that guy back, you know? Do you remember? He used to bring me flowers and even made me a playlist on my iPod once."

"Yeah, to get into your pants! Guys like that are a dime a dozen. Maybe even more like a penny a dozen. And no one even *likes* pennies! They're sleazeballs who think they can pick some flowers and make you a mix tape and then deflower the virgin."

Nora nodded and shrugged in acknowledgment. "Sometimes, I just feel like there won't be anyone else." Sniffling, she tried not to sound as pathetic as she felt, but failed miserably.

"What the hell are you talking about? I'm sorry to burst your bubble, but I am *not* going to attend this pity party. You should know by now you are nothing less than beautiful and awesome. There is a guy out there for you who will see all of that. You just need a change of scenery. Get out of this small town college crap and go on this incredible adventure!" Chloe yelled in Nora's ear as she squeezed her. "But first, I think we need to take you shopping. Get you some of your own fucking t-shirts," she berated, wrinkling her nose in distaste and tossing John's shirt in the trash bin.

Chloe was right, a change of scenery was exactly what Nora needed.

CHAPTER THREE

Nora's lack of sleep on the plane to Italy was beginning to catch up with her. Professor Hoffman moved at an impressive speed-walk through the airport she was having trouble keeping up with, practically running and weaving around other passengers and jostling a few. Tom and Judy were close behind him, but Nora was having some issues with the wheels on her luggage. One of the wheels continually got stuck, finally catching on the edge of a pillar and the offending wheel was wrenched free of its tiny axle.

"Are you kids all right back there?" Professor Hoffman shouted over his shoulder.

"No!" she yelled from behind as she stopped to examine her luggage. The wheel was nowhere to be found, giving her no discernible method to fix it. Crouching beside her luggage, the prickle and sting of warning for her oncoming tears warmed behind her eyes. This trip was not starting out how she had expected it would. Taking deep breaths to ward off the waterworks, she quickly found it was no use. Other people got 'hangry,' but she got what Chloe always called 'exhaustrated'—exhausted and frustrated. And exhaustrated *always* ended in tears.

"Goodness, Nora, are you okay?" Professor Hoffman's kind voice asked from above her.

Nora looked up, aware she was wearing her ugly-crier face, complete with red-rimmed eyes and splotchy cheeks. Shaking her head, silent tears slid down her cheeks when she rose to standing. She took deep, cleansing breaths and closed her eyes, willing the tears to subside and her composure to return.

"It's busted," Tom announced loudly, interrupting the calm Nora had drawn into herself and choking her with his ever-present cloud of cologne.

"So it would seem," Professor Hoffman observed, frowning down at the splintered plastic. "We'll improvise. Here, you can pull my luggage, and I'll carry yours," he decided with a pitying smile.

After luggage was unclipped and rearranged, Judy pulled her into a quick side-hug. "We're almost there," she reassured with a squeeze before they were off toward the exit again.

In a matter of a few minutes, they managed to find their way to the Metropolitan train to take them to the Tiburtina bus station. It was all a flurry of activity until they were finally seated on the bus with nearly four hours to go until they reached their destination.

Breathing a sigh of relief, Nora closed her eyes to calm the shaking in her limbs and ease her heartbeat back down to something less like she'd just sprinted a mile. They couldn't have been on the road for more than a few minutes before Nora was asleep.

Nora awoke with a start when the bus lurched to a stop and people began chattering all around her as they gathered their belongings and prepared to disembark. Rubbing the sleep and confusion from her eyes, she followed the example of the other passengers and gathered her backpack. Stepping from the bus, she stood with her Professor and classmates beside the other travelers while they waited patiently for stowed bags. Luckily, their group had been one of the last to board the bus, so their luggage was near the front of the compartment and came out first.

Outside the door, a woman stood holding a sign reading 'Hoffman.'

"Ah! Here we are then," Professor Hoffman remarked, speeding toward the woman.

The woman smiled when the Professor shook her hand. "Welcome to Italy, my friends. *Ciao*, I'm Giana, Mr. Micelli's assistant," the woman greeted with heavily-accented English and a broad smile. "Shall we get you to the villa?"

Without waiting for a reply, Giana headed away from the bus. The four Americans followed her to an SUV and wearily loaded the luggage into the back. Professor Hoffman slipped into the front seat while Nora piled into the back with Judy and Tom.

"Are we ready?" Giana surveyed, smiling at them in the rearview mirror.

"Yes!" Judy affirmed excitedly while Nora and Tom nodded their agreement.

"I am sorry we are not spending any time in Siena today. It is a beautiful city. Mr. Micelli has requested I bring you straight to the villa to get you settled. I am sure you all need some time to rest too," Giana observed, looking at them all in turn in the mirror, though Nora could have sworn Giana's eyes lingered on her longer than the others.

"Indeed," Professor Hoffman agreed with a nod. "Not to worry, though, we are close enough that we should be able to come and explore when there is a break in work. Make a day trip of it. How long until we arrive at the villa?"

"It is a thirty minute drive. Dinner will be waiting for you when you arrive," Giana replied with a smile. "Enjoy the view and we will talk more details after you have settled in."

Nora watched as vast farmland flew past them—fields occasionally dotted with the farms' homesteads and outbuildings. As she watched the green patchwork pass by, she realized this place was more like home than she would have imagined. Here, it was a little bit warmer than it was at home at this time of year, but if she didn't look too closely at the style of the buildings they passed—or that the plants varied from the near-arctic hardiness required to grow at home—she could almost imagine they were still in Minnesota. The mere thought of home calmed her jittery nerves, bringing a smile to her face.

Almost too soon, the drive through the countryside was over and they pulled up to the villa. Giana led them into the house where she pointed out the rooms and showed them the five apartments—one for each of them and one for the woman Mr. Micelli hired to cook and keep house for the duration of their stay. Giana pointed out a few of the house's amenities and led them back to the foyer where she bid them all farewell and informed them both she and Mr. Micelli would meet with them in the morning to discuss business. They each chose a room and dropped their luggage before descending on the food laid out on the table for them.

Nora ate with gusto and then bid her companions goodnight, although the sun was still out.

Once inside the solitude of her new home away from home, Nora collapsed on the bed without even undressing and closed her eyes.

***

Nora woke with the sun shining in her eyes and a crick in her neck. She rolled out of bed and stretched, rolling her neck from side to side. Pawing through her suitcase, she found clean clothes and toiletries then made her way to the shared bathroom. Padding across the stone floor, she closed the door as quietly as she could. She cleaned up as quickly as she could to ensure there was enough warm water for the others, though it already began dwindling by the end of her shower. There might be some conflict in sharing a bathroom with three other people.

Nora and Judy ate breakfast then chatted about the villa and exploring the yard until Professor Hoffman joined them. Their conversation turned to the dig and their speculations about what they might find. Tom barely said a word when he finally joined them. Before long, there was a knock at the door, and the housekeeper emerged from out of nowhere to let Mr. Micelli and Giana into the kitchen.

Nora was completely taken aback when she saw their benefactor. He looked nothing like the middle-aged Italian man in a dark suit and expensive loafers she had imagined. Instead, she was met with a man in his late twenties or early thirties, with light brown hair and brown eyes. Dressed casually in cargo pants and a t-shirt, his clothing showcased his muscular physique. Nora looked over at Judy.

She, too, obviously noticed he was gorgeous by the way she was self-consciously finger-combing her tangled hair.

When Tom took him in, he visibly straightened and his mouth turned up into an almost-sneer.

Professor Hoffman seemed to be the only one who didn't have a reaction to him, other than to stand and shake his hand and pull him into a man-hug, complete with the bro slap on the back.

"Professor Hoffman, so glad to see you guys made it here in one piece." Mr. Micelli laughed while he poured himself a cup of coffee. He took a quick sip and then looked around the table, appraising each of them in turn. "So, this is the team. Let's see, Tom, you're easy to pick out. And you must be Nora," he guessed, looking at Judy, "and that would make you Judy," he concluded, turning to Nora.

Judy giggled beside Nora and tucked her hair behind her ears shyly. "You got us backward, Mr. Micelli," she twittered, batting her eyelashes at him.

Nora watched Tom roll his eyes across the table.

"My apologies, *signorina*. I guess I just have to get to know you all better, so I don't mix you up again. And you can call me Dave," Mr. Micelli apologized with a wink.

"Dave," Judy answered with another giggle.

Nora was ready to kick her under the table to knock some sense back in to her.

"Shall we go over the plan?" Professor Hoffman interrupted, a slight note of irritation in his tone.

"Of course, of course." Dave sighed, placing his cup on the table. "The site is less than a mile down the road from here. You can either walk there each morning, or I have provided a golf cart for your use to travel back and forth. I am planning to turn the historic structure into a luxury spa, so I want to make sure we look around the entirety of the building as well as in areas surrounding the garden to ensure anything buried under there is unearthed *before* I begin building. I would hate to have to either stop construction or tear things up later, should there be some reason for officials involved in antiquities to question my due diligence. Now, the initial item in question is still half-buried where we found it. I didn't have anyone with the right tools or knowledge to treat the item as delicately as I believe it ought to be treated. Thus, the reason you all are here."

Professor Hoffman sat up a bit straighter with the compliment.

Dave continued, "Now, I will be visiting the site periodically while the dig is in progress, but I won't be there every day. Giana will be your day-to-day contact out there. If you need something, go to her. If you have something to report, report it to her and she'll get it to me right away. I know this is just an internship for you guys," Dave perceived, his glance sliding across all three students. "But I expect you to put in your best effort and be as efficient as possible. I don't want to drag this out forever. I intend to build by the end of the summer, so this isn't some indefinite vacation. I want the entire area around the structure examined, including the garden. Are we clear?"

Nora saw Dave's charisma give way to a shrewd businessman who expected nothing less than absolute efficiency of his employees, paid or not.

"You will work a five-day workweek, more if you deem it necessary, Professor. That should leave you plenty of time for exploration. Hell, maybe I'll even join you on some of your excursions," Dave offered, glancing over at Judy and then to Nora with a wolfish smile.

Professor Hoffman frowned. "Let's go see this artifact of yours, then," He rose from his chair and led their party from the villa and down the road.

CHAPTER FOUR

"Nora, will you kindly fetch a new shovel from that shed near the garden?" Professor Hoffman requested with a sigh as he tossed the two halves of his broken spade to the ground.

"Uh, sure," Nora replied hesitantly.

They'd been at the estate, digging along the north wall of the antique structure for nearly a week now. They'd extricated the initial artifact within the first two days of work, and now they were just digging in the general area to make sure they didn't miss any other potentially valuable items. The 'artifact' ended up being nothing more than a piece of broken pottery a few decades old, not exactly Roman, then. In all the time they'd been there, they'd avoided the garden on the other side of the building. They all felt the same creepy vibe when near it, and Nora could almost swear she had heard muffled screaming coming from there at times. Just the thought of it now gave her goose bumps.

Overactive imagination, she told herself as she slowly made her way to the south-facing expanse of stone. When the garden came into view, the hairs on the back of her neck prickled and her arms broke out in more goose bumps. An overwhelming sense of dread nearly overtook her and it required considerable effort to force her feet across the threshold of the capacious garden. She could imagine it was probably something amazing to behold in its heyday. A large cork tree stood at the center, its branches twisted and tangled unto itself from neglect of pruning. A small, wooden bistro table laid on its side, half-rotted, the matching chairs – reduced to nothing more than kindling – scattered over the marble flagstones. Nora couldn't bring herself to encroach any further into the space, getting the distinct feeling she was disturbing a hallowed place.

A far-off shout from one of her colleagues on the other side of the building stirred her from her trance. She pressed ahead to the small potting shed set in a lean-to against the main building, despite the deep feeling of foreboding which seemed to seep into her very bones.

Nora dug through the contents of the dusty building and her efforts were rewarded with two shovels. She grabbed them both, deciding if she brought the pair, then her chances of being sent back here again were greatly diminished. When she re-emerged into the sunlight, an agonizing and otherworldly scream broke through the stillness. It sounded human—almost. Nora tried to convince herself it was just the wind through some opening in the wall that would make such a noise. Despite her convincing, an instinctual urge to flee gripped her. Instead of running away, her feet remained rooted in place, her knuckles white from her death-grip on the shovels.

When another eerie, muffled, unmistakably *human* cry sounded, she sprinted toward the exit of the garden, intent on getting the hell out of there, only to find her conscience and curiosity wouldn't allow her to go any further.

What if there was someone trapped somewhere in the garden? Maybe there was an old well or something she hadn't seen and someone had fallen down it. What if someone was hurt? She certainly couldn't leave an injured person to suffer, but maybe it would be better if she got help. Mentally shaking away her cowardice, she continued to reassure herself there was nothing to be afraid of. *Stop being a coward and go help.* Someone needed her, and it might be too late for them if she ran to get her classmates. That and she wanted, no, *needed* to satisfy her curiosity and find out what that noise was. Her curiosity won out in the end and she crept toward the massive tree, thinking that was where she had heard the screams coming from. As she moved closer, the cold feeling of dread she'd felt upon entering the garden sat like a stone in her gut. When she reached the base of the tree, she heard the heart-stopping scream again and realized it was coming from the tree.

No, from *below* the tree, in the earth beneath its roots. Gasping, realization dawned on her that someone was buried there, *alive!* The thought crossed her mind that this could all be some kind of hoax, but she decided she'd rather feel foolish for being gullible enough to fall for such a prank than to leave someone to die if it wasn't someone's sick idea of a joke.

Quickly throwing one of the shovels aside, she began furiously digging with the other. How long could someone survive down there? Each inch further into the soil, she felt the dread leech further into her, gnawing at her bones. Despite the voice in her head attempting to convince her to abandon her rescue mission, she continued toiling. Sweat dripped down her back and her arms trembled with each shovelful of dirt cast aside. This was harder than she'd initially thought.

Pausing, she listened for the eerie cries from below which had been absent since she began digging. Maybe she *had* imagined it? A muffled yell coming from beneath her feet made her jump back. Well, at least she wasn't crazy.

"Tom! Judy!" Nora shouted weakly, attempting to get the attention of her classmates for help. Even with her unrelenting determination, she'd only managed to dig down six inches into the packed soil. Frowning, she stuck the shovel into the dirt again, everything about this was strange.

"Everything okay?" Tom panted as he pulled to an abrupt stop just outside the garden. "We heard you yell."

"You're going to think I'm crazy," Nora hedged. "But I keep hearing someone yelling, like they're buried down there." She pointed, to the disturbed earth at her feet.

Instead of wary, like she thought he would be, Tom appeared almost relieved. "I thought I was the only one who heard it," he admitted, taking a tentative step through the ruined gate.

"Help me?" Nora plead, barely keeping tears at bay when she handed Tom the shovel. Dread and relief warred within her, at least she wasn't crazy, but what would they find in this hole?

Another wail startled Tom just as his shovel pierced the dirt, his wide gaze snapping up to meet Nora's. Wordlessly, the two of them continued to deepen the hole Nora started.

When the hole reached a little more than a couple feet down, Nora's shovel connected with a solid surface. Scraping the spade across the wood, her stomach roiled when the outline of a coffin came into view.

Tom's worried gaze met hers. "I don't know what we'll find in there, it could be a trapped animal. Stay here, and I'll get Professor Hoffman," he ordered as he ran from the garden.

The previously animalistic sounds morphed into definitive cries of help, accompanied by the soft thud of what Nora could only assume was a fist pounding. Hearing the noise from the other side of a piece of wood spurred her into frantic action, she couldn't just stand and wait for Tom and the professor to return, she had to do something. There was a *person* down there.

"Hang on, I'll get you out of there!" she shouted, her voice cracking with emotion at the thought that some monster had buried a live person there.

Finding a split in the wood of the lid, Nora wedged the shovel in it and twisted. The wood was more rotted than she had expected and gave way with surprisingly little effort. Dropping to her hands and knees, Nora tore desperately at the decaying wood until a large piece broke off. Tossing it to the side, she was ready to comfort and reassure the unfortunate soul beneath it.

Any words of reassurance died on her lips when her gaze rested on the sight of a figure more dead than alive lying in the coffin. The person appeared almost as though they'd been mummified, like something out of a museum display, with gray skin, sunken eyes and tufts of hair missing. It reminded her of a scene from the movie *Seven*, one which had always given her nightmares. She shook off the chill running down her spine, wondering if the body was even real.

When she leaned forward to get a better look, the corpse before her opened its eyes.

Such cold, blue eyes.

"Oh my God," she gasped, a small sob escaping her.

Nora let out a scream when the figure lunged at her from the coffin, faster than she imagined someone so emaciated could move. It had an impressive grip on her throat with one hand and the other tangled in her hair. Nora tried to scream again and was met with excruciating pain in her neck accompanied by the agony of tearing flesh and warm liquid spilling from the wound.

Scrabbling for purchase on the caving wood beneath her, she attempted to push away from her attacker. The pressure of her blood being siphoned from her with every swallow the creature took was the only thread keeping her tethered to reality while the pain clouding her mind made it nearly impossible to register what was actually happening to her.

Blood loss left Nora drowsy and it took a few seconds to realize she was on her back now, staring up into the blurry branches from beneath the tree. I must have lost my glasses, she thought absently as blurry shapes moved above her with the breeze. A pitch-black crow sat perched above her in the tree, cawing a mocking warning that was much too late. Or maybe he was waiting to escort her soul to the underworld. That's what crows did, didn't they? Though she thought it was far more likely, he was calling his friends to dinner as he watched her slide farther from life.

Somehow, Nora felt calm as death loomed over her. She had to admit the grim reaper was far more attractive than she'd imagined, with bright blue eyes and golden locks. He really was good looking, to die for, even. She let out a gurgling chuckle through the torn flesh of her throat at her dark humor when she was literally looking death in the eyes. Death bent toward her and she closed her eyes, waiting to experience the sensation of having her soul separated from her body.

CHAPTER FIVE

Endre stared down at the mangled woman, who, literally laughed in the face of her impending doom before her eyes fluttered closed, giving her the countenance of sleep. She had not long left in this world, and he had to decide if he wished to save her or abandon her to perish. Even without his attack, she would have died in a matter of months. The sickness coursing through her veins carried an unmistakable taste of doom.

It was her green eyes, so much like Ingrid's which pierced through the primal hunger to feed and kept him from making the kill. It was his curiosity about this woman who laughed at the very visage of death which prompted him to slit his wrist with a sharp fang and drizzle blood into her open mouth. His blood would prolong her life for a time. Keeping her heart pumping would at least give him leave to decide her ultimate fate. With the hunger still gnawing at his guts, he could barely form a coherent thought, let alone make a life or death decision for another.

The scent of humans nearby floated to him on the wind, twisting his insides. Bloodlust roared through him, sharpening his senses, honing them to better stalk his prey. It would be no real hunt, though, if these humans proved to be as defenseless as the woman he already drank from. The woman who continued to draw his gaze, breaking into the need to feed like nothing he had ever felt before.

Prying his attention from the lovely creature at his feet, Endre assessed his surroundings. The humans were nearly upon him. Three heartbeats pounded in his ears, more blood to glut himself on than he'd had in nearly a century. The darkest corners of his being roared to life, crowding out logic and reason, demanding he kill to survive. For a hundred years, he had relied on that abyss within to remain alive and faced with the prospect of full regeneration, he was powerless to hold the wave of darkness at bay when it washed over him.

CHAPTER SIX

Nora tried to force her eyes open but the blinding light behind her eyelids was excruciating. Her head pounded and she couldn't remember if she was hungover or not. No, that wasn't it. She didn't remember drinking. Her heart stilled for a beat when the memory of opening the coffin in the garden hit her. It was nearly certain the image of that *thing* sinking its teeth into her carotid artery would haunt her for the rest of her days.

A deep voice murmured above her, the sound smooth and smoky, sending a delightful tremble through her limbs.

It took a moment to realize the voice was speaking to her, though she had no idea what it was saying. Cracking her eyelids to search for the source, she immediately regretted it. The brightness seared her irises and shot pain to her already pulsing head. Taking deep breaths, she attempted to quell the nausea rolling through her.

The voice spoke again, the tone calming, and the only word she caught was *bellissima.*

The bright light dimmed, a shadow blocking some of the sun's illumination. Nora slowly opened her eyes, little by little, taking in the blurry figure hovering above her. The nausea subsided and the pounding in her head dulled, replaced by warmth radiating through her limbs, and seemingly concentrated in her more intimate areas. As her vision sharpened, the face of the most impossibly handsome man she'd ever seen leaned over her. His ice blue gaze roamed over her face and studied her eyes while hers took in the chiseled lines of his jaw with a hint of stubble and the golden blond hair hanging just past his ears. It was like the movie god Thor had just stepped out of the screen.

She was drunk. Or maybe she hit her head. Or maybe she was dead and there was a heaven, where they have angels who look like movie gods.

"*Bellissima,*" he murmured as he brushed a lock of hair out of her eyes.

Nora licked her dry lips and opened them to speak, watching as his eyes flicked down to her mouth. "Who—" she started, swallowed against the dryness in her throat, and tried again, "Who are you?"

"Ah, so it is English then. That will make things easier, my Italian is a tad rusty," he affirmed with a slight accent she couldn't quite place—but it didn't sound Italian to her. He stood and paced as he appraised her.

Nora noted the deep furrow of a scowl line his brow.

"American?" he queried.

Nora nodded dumbly; her throat raw, but she instantly regretted the movement when the pounding in her head returned.

The angel sighed. "No wonder you do not speak Italian in Italy," he scolded, shaking his head.

Nora craned her neck painfully to keep him in her line of sight as he sauntered toward her.

Crouching down, he spoke low into her ear, "I despise Americans. Arrogant, greedy, and useless. Perhaps I should finish you after all. But I thought you might prove to be useful. I suppose even an immortal can be wrong from time to time."

Fear spiked through her, piercing the sensation that she now realized was arousal. *Finish* her? What did *that* mean? Her brain attempted to process a thousand explanations all at once and settled on the terrifying reality that somehow this vision hovering dangerously over her head, ready to snuff out the life she thought she'd already lost, was the same creature she'd unearthed. Glancing down from his face to his soiled and tattered clothing, nearly rotted away by time, her worst fears were confirmed. Closing her eyes, she braced herself for the bite or the blow or whatever sinister method he had devised to dispatch her. She held her breath with anticipation, but the expected pain never came.

"What is your name, *Bellissima* American?"

His voice rumbled next to her ear, his hot breath skittering across her skin. The sensation sent liquid heat pooling between her thighs. Opening her eyes, she found his blue ones boring into her expectantly. Her heart pounded in her chest, and she wasn't sure if it was from her fear or his nearness. "Nora. Eleanora," she managed to croak hoarsely from her burning throat.

The angel of death chuckled and stood, giving Nora room to breathe again. "Well, Light One, it is appropriate then, that you have freed me from my dark prison. So I will let you live. For now," he admitted, circling back to stand at her side so she didn't have to twist her neck to see him.

When she gave him a puzzled expression, he sighed and reprimanded with mock sadness, "Americans, you choose names without regard to meaning. Your name means 'light,' Eleanora. I have decided to spare you, only because I need something from you. Never mistake my actions for kindness or mercy. Those human tendencies left me long ago."

He left her lying on the floor, still paralyzed and reeling from nearly dying and then being spared, as he rummaged around nearby.

Nora turned her head to watch him pull the clothing off of another figure on the ground. As he jostled the body to remove the garment, she caught glimpses of the face and realized the bloody and mangled corpse was her professor. It was only with that truly gruesome visual did reality finally sink in.

Bile rose up in her throat. Nora quickly rolled to her side and vomited, staring in abject horror at the pool of red. Blood. There was blood in her vomit. Maybe she was dying after all.

"It is not your blood, it is mine," her captor simply stated without turning from removing the professor's clothing,

As if that made it somehow more comforting, knowing his blood was in her stomach.

Standing, he unabashedly shed his tattered rags, revealing the body of an Adonis, and Nora felt her blood—or was it his?—rush to her cheeks and her core at the same time. He was an exquisite specimen, and even though she knew him to be a monster, that didn't stop her from admiring his physique. By the time her eyes took in every inch of him, she was practically drooling.

Standing naked as a jaybird, he smirked down at her open-mouthed expression.

As he began pulling on her professor's clothing, reality—what little of it Nora felt like she was still holding on to—slammed back into her. Professor Hoffman was dead, and the *thing* in front of her had killed him. She dry heaved, her stomach now empty, and remembered his blood in her vomit.

"What are you?" she asked hoarsely.

"I am made of the things which roam your worst nightmares, Eleanora. I am immortal, a creature of darkness. First called *Draugr*. Call me what you will, but I was last referred to as a Vampire," he stated, buttoning his newly acquired jeans.

"Your— your blood—am I going to turn into a…" Nora swallowed to rid her mouth of the acrid taste of blood and vomit, "…Vampire?"

He pulled on a soiled white t-shirt which stretched over his sculpted chest. "No, the process is more complicated than that. I needed your blood to regenerate so I can feed from you, and you needed my blood to heal, so I fed it to you. Besides, I need to keep you human," he explained with a condescending chuckle, gazing down at the stained shirt with some measure of disgust.

"What are you going to do with me?" Nora whispered, her body quaking with terror.

"I am going to feed from you, and you are going to help me exact my revenge. When I no longer have need of you, I will kill you. What year is it?" he inquired, too casual for someone who just told her he was going to keep her prisoner, drink her blood, and then kill her.

"2015," she whispered, a tremor in her voice.

"Ninety-two years," he murmured, more to himself than her, frowning as he pulled on a steel-toed boot.

When he finished dressing, he looked more like an archaeologist than a remorseless killer. When he strode across the space toward her, his movements were more feline than human, too full of grace for someone dressed in jeans and steel-toed boots. Bending at the waist, he hauled her to her feet into his arms with nearly no effort.

The sudden movement and his hands on her made Nora dizzy, nauseous and aroused all at the same time. Leaning her against the wall, he turned to retrieve a water bottle. Nora's weak muscles protested the lack of support and she went crashing toward the ground.

Before she hit the stone, she collided with his hard chest instead.

Leaning with her cheek pressed to his hardened muscles, she attempted to catch her breath and willed the vertigo to subside. Nora was suddenly acutely aware of her arms wrapped around his waist and his shirt bunched tightly in her fists at his back. His skin was warm through the cotton beneath her cheek and she wondered how he could feel so warm if he was dead.

His hands slid up her sides and a shiver ran through her as his fingertips grazed the sides of her breasts. Nora wished his hands would explore her further, but they didn't. Instead, he grasped her shoulders and pulled her away from his heat. She missed it immediately. She had to wonder if along with her blood, she had also lost her sanity.

Maybe she was in shock. Traumatized. He was a killer, a Vampire, her captor, and all she could think about was wanting his naked flesh pressed against hers, wanting him inside her.

It's official, I've lost my mind.

Carefully, more so than she would have expected, he guided her to sit on the ground and leaned her against the wall. The cool stone did nothing to quench the heat burning across her skin. Nora's vision blurred and swam and she closed her eyes to make the movement stop. A moment later, something cold and hard pressed against her lips then she felt the blessed water drip into her mouth and dribble down her chin. Opening her mouth, she took long swallows of the reviving liquid. Then the cool water was gone as her mouth was filled with a warm, metallic tang.

Her eyes flew open when she realized what it was. The Vampire had his wrist pressed against her mouth, feeding her his blood. She sputtered and turned her face away, spitting the blood on the floor.

In the flash of fractions of a second, he had her lying on her back. "You are weak, Eleanora, you need my blood to heal."

"No," Nora protested with a pathetic whine, though she suspected her refusal would not stop him.

He straddled her hips and had one hand clenching her jaw, hard, his bloody wrist pressed to her lips. Nora kept her lips pressed together tightly and tried to move her face away, knowing it was a futile attempt. Snarling above her, he tightened his grip on her jaw. The pain was excruciating, and on reflex, Nora opened her mouth to scream, but nothing came out before her mouth filled with the coppery liquid again.

Flailing her arms, she tried to bat his hands away, but he was much too strong. She refused to swallow and soon her mouth was filled nearly to overflowing with his blood. When she tried to spit it back at him, he realized her intention and removed his bleeding wrist from her mouth then plugged her nose.

"Swallow it, Eleanora. You need it to heal," he growled at her.

Nora held her breath until black spots danced at the edges of her vision.

"My blood is already in your veins, Eleanora. You belong to me now and you *will* do as I command," he snarled, inches from her face.

The black spots began to spread and darkness bled from the edges of her vision, threatening to take her under. But she still resisted. When she had nearly blacked out, her body gave in and swallowed without her permission. She took in a deep, shuddering breath, soothing the burning in her lungs.

He still held her jaw tightly, and leaned in so they were mere inches apart. The icy pools of his eyes glared into hers. "I own you now, Eleanora, do not forget it," he whispered harshly, his breath blowing across her lips, sending a shiver through her.

Their mouths were so close, and Nora had an unexplainable urge to tilt her jaw to close the gap. Her heart hammered in her chest, flushing her skin and accelerating her breathing.

The Vampire gave her a wolfish smile and leaned in closer, almost giving her what she so unreasonably wanted. His tongue darted out and licked the blood from her bottom lip.

Nora exhaled a small, unbidden moan. He made another pass with his tongue over her upper lip, and Nora was sure she would spontaneously combust if he didn't press his mouth to hers.

"I see my pheromones work quite nicely on you, Eleanora. The blood serves to strengthen them. This is how we catch our prey, you see. I become irresistible to you, even when you know exactly what I am, even after I have told you that you will die before our time together is through," he whispered, speaking to her lips, just a hairsbreadth from touching them. "But I am not going to give you the pleasure you want. I do not play with my food."

He released his painful hold on her jaw and stood, leaving her on the ground, his blood now coursing through her body—her desire to have more of him unsated.

CHAPTER SEVEN

Endre watched from a short distance as flames engulfed the building which had been his home so long ago. Once it was gone, it would be the last remnant of his life here. He could move on and there would be nothing left to leave behind. In all his years, in his many lifetimes, this place was the one home where he had truly felt at peace since his human life was taken from him. But then it had become his tomb, his never-ending nightmare for decades. A part of him felt sadness knowing that in the morning, it would be nothing more than ashes and a charred pile of rubble. The other part of him, however, felt a profound sense of vindication burning his prison to the ground, and he only wished he could burn the resulting ashes into nothingness.

The woman, Eleanora, stirred at his feet, reminding him of the need to move on. The blaze was large and would soon attract attention. Attention he did not want focused on him. Pulling her to her feet, he supported her weight as she slumped limply against him. She was still weak. He had drained nearly every drop from her at their first encounter. A few mouthfuls of his blood would not fully restore her, this was evident. Soon, she would need more of his blood to keep her heart beating.

Guilt gnawed at him. In his the dark haze of his bloodlust, he had not given her companions a second thought. It would have been more merciful if he had ended her life as well. Killing the innocent was not how he preferred to do things, but then again, it had been so long since he had really been himself. The dark eternity underground with his life drifting away at an agonizing pace had nearly driven him mad. Or maybe he had it all wrong, and he *was* mad. Taking the woman on as a companion almost certainly proved he was out of his mind.

A glance down at her placid face reminded him that there was something about her which pulled him further from the edge of the abyss he had spent every moment of the last century avoiding succumbing to. Light One, indeed.

A moan sounded from her, her eyelids fluttering and a furrow formed between her brows. She was in pain. Pain he had put her through. Quickly, he forced back the guilt, lest it drag him under and leave him vulnerable to the primal darkness once again. Later. He could work on mending his fractured state of mind once he had fed Eleanora more blood.

But not here in the open, where anyone concerned with the raging inferno before him could see what he was doing. There had to be a dwelling nearby, somewhere she and her companions had been lodging. They had not been staying in the manor, of that he was certain. He had scoured the building before lighting the match, and found no evidence to indicate any people dwelled there. Quite the contrary, actually. The house appeared as though it had been abandoned quite some time ago and was in a frightful state of disrepair.

Endre could not say he was surprised at the abandonment—considering the disturbance, he created below ground when some hapless insect or rodent would happen upon his coffin and provide him with enough sustenance to call attention to his grave.

Holding the woman away from his chest, her head lolled to the side. He gave her a slight shake and her eyes opened a slit. "Eleanora, where are your lodgings?" he prompted, attempting to peer into her barely open eyes.

She mumbled something incoherently and her body slackened again.

Letting out an irritated sigh, he shook her again, with a little more force this time. "Eleanora, your room, where is it?"

Her eyes snapped open and then slowly dropped closed again.

Endre pulled in a deep breath to stifle his irritation and the sudden urge to snap her neck. The dark thought startled him enough to rein in his irritation. Clearly, it would be a struggle to fight the urge to allow his Vampire nature to take control.

He could not allow that to happen, he needed this human.

"Down the road," she whispered in slurred words.

'Down the road' was not much to go on, but the road only went two directions. His chances were fifty-fifty he would go the right direction and then he did not even know what building he was looking for or how far away it was. Right now, though, it did not matter which way he chose. Sirens in the distance heralded the arrival of the human authorities, and although he had no fear of the humans, their attempt to detain him would only create more of a delay and more bloodshed. He had taken three lives today, nearly four, to replenish his body. Any more would be merely gluttonous. It would simply be best to avoid further contact with humans—with the exception of his charge, of course.

Scooping the woman into his arms, Endre headed toward a copse of trees. Perhaps he could give her some more blood in the near-privacy of the trees and get a better answer from her on their destination. As he walked, her head bounced from the lack of support and her arms flailed in all directions before he adjusted his grip. It had been over a thousand years since he'd been human, he had forgotten how fragile they could be.

Endre made it to the stand of trees as the first automobile pulled up to the flaming building. It took considerable effort to tear his attention from the orange glow illuminating the darkening sky, and then the automobile. He had been buried quite some time, and it was clear that a significant amount had changed during his absence, as evidenced by the appearance of the vehicle.

The roar and deafening crack of the second floor of his house collapsing reminded him he was still in danger of being discovered. Glancing down at the woman in his arms, his gaze was drawn to her exposed, vulnerable throat. The pulsing of her heart's sluggish beat in her carotid had slowed since his last observation. If he did not supply her with more blood, she would surely expire. His growing guilt simply would not accept her death as a viable outcome of today's events.

Letting out a drawn sigh, Endre placed the woman on the ground and provided her with a few more mouthfuls of blood. Frustration settled over him as he observed the slow increase in her heartrate. Perhaps it was the illness destroying her body which required more blood to heal. In all his long years, he had never encountered a human who required so much nourishment to remain coherent, even after being nearly drained.

Endre supposed he could thank the Norns, those meddling Nordic goddesses of fate, for such an intrusion into his life, sending him a woman to save him with such a close likeness to his beloved Ingrid. There was a lesson in here, he was sure of it, though its riddle had yet to reveal itself to him.

Not long after the fresh infusion of his blood, Endre was able to get more information on a direction and name of the villa at which she had been staying. This time, as he quickly walked them to the house, he slung her over his shoulder like a sack of grain when she lost consciousness again. The need to find a way to replenish her sickened body weighed heavily on him. Though carrying her was not a burden for his strength, he was concerned with the rapid deterioration. Clearly, her body was not manufacturing blood fast enough. That did not bode well for his plan to feed from her exclusively, rather than hunting in the open while formulating his plans for revenge.

When Endre strode into the room she indicated was hers, he laid her onto the bed and took in the small space. It was clearly temporary lodging, with only a bed and a small table beside it to furnish the room, not even a chest of drawers. Her luggage lay open on the floor with everything still neatly packed inside. It appeared as though she had just arrived, though he had heard her and the other humans working, digging, for days.

Rifling through her suitcase, he found nothing of much interest. Clothes and a few books, nothing he had ever heard of, modern literature, he supposed. Then he saw her handbag on the table. He attempted to dig through it, but to no avail. There were so many things tucked into the small bag, he could barely fit his hand in there. He opted, instead, to upend the purse and dump its contents into the middle of the floor. It was a wonder so much could fit in so small a space.

Sifting through the contents, he found her wallet containing money and a device which glowed and showed the time when he pressed buttons on it. So much of what was scattered on the floor he was unfamiliar with, affirming his need for guidance from the frail human still passed out cold on the bed.

Endre peered out the window at the ever-darkening sky. They would only have a short respite before the authorities came here looking for the girl. In this small community, the locals would all know a team of Americans was working at the manor which now served as their funeral pyre, and the locals would surely also know where they were staying. It would only be a matter of time before someone came calling, and they could not very well still be here when that happened.

Venturing from room to room, he ransacked the belongings of his latest victims, a pit growing in his stomach as he did so. Killing innocents had never been his way, but a century of isolation tends to alter one's perception of the world. As his body wasted away, so did his compass.

With blood once again flowing through him, his mind and body fought for precedence. His body screamed the siren song of survival, which can only be achieved with blood with no regard for the source. His mind portrayed a quieter, but growing voice of reason, formulating arguments for returning to the evolved mindset that humans were not merely cattle to be slaughtered for sustenance. Although, with each glance at Eleanora, Endre remained unsure if it was his mind or his body which allowed her to live.

When he returned to the woman, she had not so much as moved a muscle since he had placed her there. Checking the time on his new watch, he noted they had already dawdled here for nearly a half-hour. By his estimations, they were almost out of time, and he was most definitely out of patience.

Huffing out an irritated sigh for no one's benefit but his own, Endre approached the bed. He stared down at the woman, contorted into a pile of limbs where he had dropped her. The position appeared quite uncomfortable, one of her arms bent at an unnatural angle. He really must take more care to keep her from injury. It would not do to have to continue to repair her broken body with blood from his own. As it was, the current cycle they were on would not last forever. If he hoped to restore both of them to full health, more blood would be needed.

More humans would die. Unfortunately, it had been far too long since he had been required to exhibit restraint when feeding. It was a skill he would need to re-learn. If he hoped to feed from Eleanora without killing her, he would need to practice. Taking in the state of her still–unconscious form, he estimated it would be some time before he would be feeding from her again.

A voice in the back of his mind whispered once again, *What the Hel am I doing with her? If she cannot provide me with sustenance and cannot stay conscious enough to guide me, then why continue the charade?*

Perhaps it was the pang in his chest where he was sure he was no longer capable of feeling anything.

With the decision made to continue toting the human along with him, Endre rearranged her body more comfortably and gave her another dose of blood. While he gave the liquid time to make its way into her system, he kept himself busy by packing the belongings he had strewn about the floor into her luggage. He growled in frustration when he noticed it appeared one of the wheels was broken. As he moved to retrieve the luggage from one of the other dead, he heard the woman stir.

Finally.

"How'd I get here?" Her hoarse voice came from behind him.

He turned to find her struggling to sit up and gazing curiously at him with unfocused eyes.

"Good, you're finally awake," he snapped with a snarl. Dammit, he did not intend to lash out at her.

She looked taken aback and shrank back into the bed.

Endre let his gaze roam over her, making a clinical assessment and keeping his gaze from focusing on the more alluring parts of her body. She would need to clean up and change clothing if they were going to travel unnoticed. A woman covered in blood would surely draw some attention.

"Here," he coaxed, holding out his hand to her. "You need to clean up."

She gazed down at her hands, covered in dried blood. Her eyes grew wide and her hands began to tremble. A small whimper escaped from her.

Due to his enhanced hearing, Endre heard both her heartrate and breathing increase rapidly. She did not move, only stared at her stained hands and whimpered. He should have anticipated she might go into shock. He did not want to be callous, but he simply did not have the time to deal with it.

Gripping her shoulders roughly, he gave her a hard shake. Her eyes snapped to his, but looking at him instead of her hands only seemed to bring on a new wave of hysteria. He gave her another swift shake which stopped the whimpering. It took considerable effort to remind himself to be careful not to snap her spine.

"Eleanora, you must get cleaned up. We need to leave. Immediately," he commanded sternly.

He pulled her to her feet, and when she faltered, he swept her up into his arms and carried her to the bathroom. She pushed weakly against him, protesting his handling. Endre ignored the protest and set her in the bathtub. He turned on the shower above her and she let out a shriek at the cold water. He could not help the crooked smile that lifted the corners of his lips at the sound. At least she was no longer producing the heart-wrenching whimper.

The cold water seemed to free her from her panic attack and she reached for the dials to add hot water. She let out a small sigh as steam rose all around them to fill the small space. He hauled her to her feet and steadied her, still unsure if she could stand on her own. The water soaked through her clothing and clung to her skin. His eyes appraised her toned form, appreciating the strength he saw in her beautiful body.

"Wash up," he ordered and folded his arms, attempting to ignore the stirring in his groin that he denied was arousal. It had been centuries since a human woman had elicited such a response from him. It was cruel of the Norns to send him a rescuer who would only serve to distract him from his purpose.

CHAPTER EIGHT

Nora looked up at the Vampire with wide eyes, trying to decipher if he intended to leave her in privacy, or if he expected her to strip naked in front of him. He stood with his arms crossed and his cold, unyielding eyes boring into hers. When she made no move to undress, he gave a low growl deep in his throat that shot a spike of fear through her.

She decided to start with washing her hair, face and hands—anywhere she could see blood. When she finished, she reached to turn off the water but was met with another growl.

"Undress," he demanded, heat flickering in his eyes.

Nora hesitated before she brought shaking hands to the hem of her t-shirt. She turned her back to him, looking for some sliver of privacy, of modesty.

"Face me," he ordered, his voice thick and almost pained.

Nora closed her eyes and turned back so she was facing him. She kept her eyes tightly closed as she quickly pulled off her shirt and stripped out of her jeans. When she stood—shivering despite the hot water—in only her bra and underwear, she heard him let out a barely audible groan. The sound sent a thrill through her, her body warming under his attention. Opening her eyes, she found him still staring at her, but the coldness from earlier was replaced with heat and hunger.

As if sensing her perceptions of his reaction, he stepped away from the tub and pulled the shower curtain closed between them. "I have no interest in your body, woman. Finish up," he called as the door closed behind him.

Nora wondered who he was trying to convince, because there was no mistaking the 'interest' in his gaze.

The warmth from his perusal drained from her almost as quickly as it sprang up, and she was thankful. She did not want to be attracted to this monster, but always felt a growing ache deep within when he was near. In her haze, she remembered he had said something about pheromones. That explained the attraction to him when she should have been terrified out of her mind. Biology and chemistry—that was why her body wanted him, despite her mind's protestations.

It had absolutely nothing to do with the fact he was absolutely gorgeous with an amazing body.

Absolutely nothing. He was a killer who drank her blood.

Nora wrapped her arms around herself to quell the violent tremors shaking her body. Taking several deep breaths to calm her nerves, she quickly finished cleaning up, leaving her bra and underwear firmly in place. She kept her thoughts on the small movements required to get clean and only let her mind wander to the next step in the process. If she let her mind drift to the grisly events of earlier that day or to speculation on what her future held, and how long that future might be, she would shatter into a million little pieces.

CHAPTER NINE

Pulling the door closed behind him, Endre let out a shuddering breath as he squeezed his eyes shut to block out the image of Nora's wet body, her clothing plastered to her skin. It did not work and only served to push the visage more forcefully to the front of his mind. Godsdammit, this was not going as planned.

Tires crunching over gravel sounded from the front of the house, drawing Endre's attention from his thoughts of the enticing woman on the other side of the door he now leaned against. Someone was here.

With quick steps, Endre sped to the front of the villa, peeking through the window to catch a glimpse of the automobile. A blue and white vehicle with the words *Polizia* emblazoned across the side was parked, its flashing blue lights reflecting off the window panes.

"Godsdammit," Endre swore under his breath.

The Italian police were far more responsive than he had imagined. By his previous calculations, he should have had at least twenty more minutes to get the woman out of the house. However, the arrival of the car may prove opportune. Endre had been planning on skulking away in the dark on foot until he found a vehicle they could commandeer. This way, they would not have to search for a vehicle.

An abrupt knock sounded on the door, followed by the muffled command, spoken in Italian.

Plans and scenarios raced through Endre's mind as he attempted to grasp one that would work, but light footsteps descending from a staircase leading to an upper level startled him. Turning to the stairway, he caught a glimpse of a surprised middle aged woman. The housekeeper. How the Hel had he not heard the woman moving around above them? It had never occurred to him to search the upper level of the villa for additional occupants.

Swiftly, Endre moved toward her, intent on preventing her from alerting the police outside he was there. Without the element of surprise, he would not be able to carry out his plan to avoid an altercation by stunning the officer and merely take the vehicle—rather than killing him.

The woman's eyes grew wide and a scream left her lips before Endre's hand slapped over her mouth to block the sound.

The officer shouted before forcing the door open and stepping into Endre's view. His gaze immediately zeroed in on where Endre held the housekeeper captive, and he reached for a firearm at his side.

The sight of the gun flipped a switch somewhere deep in Endre, forcing his survival instincts to the forefront. Tossing the woman to the side, he leapt for the officer, reaching him as he squeezed off a shot. The boom echoed off the walls of the villa, far too loud for Endre's sensitive ears.

With wide terrified eyes, the officer aimed again, but Endre was on him before he could squeeze the trigger again.

A few practiced and deft movements had the officer on his knees, his gun now in Endre's hand.

Raising his arm, Endre prepared to knock the officer unconscious, but his arm hung motionless in the air when the scent of blood wafted into his nostrils. Gritting his teeth, he attempted to keep his focus on the officer. Perspiration dotted his hairline as he fought against the primal urge to feed. Quicker than he liked to admit, his self-control and logic slipped away, leaving him with only instinct.

Red clouded his vision, the color of the cursed blood calling to the *Draugr* part of him and shutting out the human logic he clung to tightly. In an instant, he plunged his fangs into the throat of the officer, draining his blood and stealing his life. A low guttural moan rose from the back of Endre's throat as he drank down mouthful after mouthful, glutting himself on the officer's life.

A terrified squeak came from the injured woman behind Endre, drawing his attention from the now-empty man. Focused eyes locked in on the red blooming from the gunshot wound in woman's thigh.

It was as if Endre were outside his body, watching as his Vampire instincts possessed his movements. Pushing back, he fought for control, but only succeeded in delaying the inevitable. Even as he drew blood from the housekeeper, he fought against that invisible force inside him. It had been so long since he had been unable rein in the urge to feed, every minute inch of control he managed to take hold of was more effort than he could ever remember expending in the past. Too long had he lived as a monster in the ground, his humanity lying dormant, allowing his instincts to keep him alive.

Rising to his feet, Endre swiped at the blood on his lips with his tongue. He had drained five humans today, almost six, and yet he still did not feel sated. That was the trap of the blood. Feeding begot more feeding, driving him into a frenzy. Before Lorenzo's betrayal and Endre's burial, he had learned to master his bloodlust until he no longer had to with the advent of his cure. Some Vampires were much better at learning to harness their need for blood than others. For him, he had viewed it like any other skill he learned, and mastered it quickly. Experiencing himself so far removed from the ability to keep from gorging himself on humans was unnerving.

Eyes closed, he drew in deep breaths, forcing down the urge to seek out more blood. The sound of the shower running filled his ears and the image of Eleanora, wet beneath the spray of water, popped into his mind again. A different brand of lust clouded his mind, driving him to take something entirely different than blood from her.

No.

Endre's eyes popped open, dulling the siren call of his combined urges for blood and flesh alike. The darkness was not gone entirely, he could still feel its cruel edge sharp along his self-control, but for the moment, he was more man than monster. It would take time to re-train his mind to keep the darkness at bay.

The sudden loss of the sound of running water drew his attention down the hall to the bathroom door, reminding him of his purpose...to get Eleanora cleaned up so they would be less conspicuous during their journey to find Lorenzo. Endre's gaze traveled down at his own blood-smeared clothing, then to the body of the police officer. Regret sank heavy in his gut, even as he attempted to push it away. There was nothing he could do now, only keep moving forward.

Time to wipe away the evidence of his sins.

CHAPTER TEN

While Nora finished washing up and drying off as best she could with her soaked undergarments on, her eyes continued to drift to the tiny window above the toilet, thoughts of escape fresh in her mind. A few quick calculations reminded her that *if* she even made it through the window, she wouldn't make it much farther. She'd seen the Vampire move, and even if she weren't so weak, he would catch her without much effort. Dread filled her when she glanced at the door, she had no other option but to do what he said. Nora didn't have a single shred of control in this situation. Every plan, every action would be immediately thwarted by the monster on the other side of that panel of wood.

Wrapping the towel up around her chest, Nora grabbed her toiletry bag and made for the door. A glance in the mirror struck her immobile for a moment. She hardly recognized the woman staring back at her. Dripping wet hair framed her ghostly pale face, green eyes wide with fear. She looked more wraith than woman, but at least she was no longer covered in blood.

Nora ran a hand over the faded scar at her neck which was a life-threatening laceration only this morning. Had it only been half a day since she lay dying in the garden? Leaning closer, she squinted to get a better look at the almost invisible wound. It had been there, there was no way she could have imagined that kind of pain. Reaching to push her glasses up her nose to sharpen the image, she realized she wasn't wearing them. Her glasses weren't on, but she could see as well as if they were. If she were a betting woman, she'd bet it had to do with the Vampire's blood. Obviously, it had tremendous healing properties which knit skin, muscles, and nerves back together quickly. It would stand to reason her eyesight could be improved too. Focusing her gaze on her own eyes, she shivered at the blank stare of the woman looking back at her. That woman should be in hysterics, at least a blubbering mass on the floor.

The door opened behind her, snapping her gaze to the reflection of the Vampire.

Huh, so, the myth about reflections wasn't true.

"It is time to go," he ordered, reaching for her arm.

Nora shrank back from his grip, clutching at the towel wrapped around her.

Frustration furrowed his brows, a frown pulled down the corners of his mouth.

Her gaze drifted down to his new outfit. Acid roiled in her stomach when she contemplated the short list of whose clothing he wore.

With a not so gentle grip, he took her arm and steered her from the bathroom toward her bedroom.

Nora stumbled along, trying to keep up with his brisk pace, but her limbs weren't quite getting the message to walk.

Pushing her roughly through the doorway of the bedroom, he barked out another order, "Get dressed." Then slammed the door behind him.

The surprise force of his push coupled with the wobbling in her legs sent her careening toward the bed where she barely managed to get her footing before she bounced off the mattress to the floor. Clutching at the terrycloth wrapped around her, Nora drew in deep breaths to calm the frantic beat of her heart.

Hands shaking, she pushed up to stand, eyeing the outfit laid out on the comforter. Her gaze jumped from the bed to where her now-absent luggage had been, and then to the window. Just like in the bathroom, it was a long shot, the idea of escaping through there.

Enormous, even. But she had to try, didn't she? At least she knew she could fit through this opening.

Half a dozen shaking steps brought her before the panes of glass, and as quietly as she could, she flipped the latch and gently tugged at the sash. It didn't budge. Straining her arms, she put more force into her effort and was rewarded with the squeal of swollen wood scraping against itself, the sound so loud it stopped her heart for a beat.

He had to have heard that.

She hadn't even had a chance to jump back from the window before the Vampire was striding through the door.

A dangerous expression clouded his features, his blue eyes the color of an angry sea. "We do not have time for this," he announced, taking purposeful strides toward her.

On instinct, Nora backed away from him until her knees hit the mattress.

The Vampire's brooding form towered over her as he pressed forward, his body so close to touching hers. "Time is of the essence. I will give you two options. You either dress without delay, or I can end your misery right here, right now. I am running out of patience."

Swallowing hard, Nora stared up into his cold eyes, debating which was the preferable choice.

His eyes narrowed at her delay in response.

"Dressed," she whispered, her eyes darting between his, attempting to decipher which was his preferred choice.

"Good," he proclaimed, taking a step back and turning for the door.

Nora's breath left her in a whoosh, and she sank to the mattress when he strode out into the hallway – leaving the door open. With shaking hands, she dropped the towel to the floor and peeled off her wet underthings – keeping her eye on the doorway. As she pulled on the dry t-shirt and jeans he left for her, the trembling in her hands subsided a bit. She'd barely finished pulling on her shoes when he reappeared in the doorway.

"Your bags are in the vehicle, let us depart," he said, gripping her arm again as he pulled her from the room.

She didn't think to protest or convey her displeasure at being manhandled. Instead, her brow furrowed in confusion. "Where are we going?"

He didn't answer. Instead, he pulled her toward the door.

Nora stumbled over something on the floor, the Vampire dragging her along. When she looked over her shoulder, she couldn't hold back a scream when she realized it was a body.

Another dead in his wake. How long before she was a lifeless body on the floor?

Struggling, she attempted to break the Vampire's grip, but her resistance was pointless. He was *much* stronger than her.

Nora couldn't tear her eyes from the blank, glassy stare of his latest victim, the features frozen in death. He'd done that. He'd killed that man and now the Vampire was kidnapping her, forcing her to go with him so one day—he could do the same to her.

Twisting in his grip, she only succeeded in giving herself bruises and drawing a frustrated growl from him. She tried to drag her feet and hit him, but he sidestepped her then eventually picked her up and carried her, screaming and fighting with everything she was worth the entire way. Nora was vaguely surprised he hadn't subdued her or killed her right there—wasn't that what a monster would do?

When they got to the car, she realized with a sinking feeling it was a police car. He'd murdered a police officer. There truly was no hope of rescue now. Not that she'd had much faith there would be. Even if the monsters from her favorite books and movies were real, it didn't mean the heroes who stopped them were. There was no hero stepping from the shadows to help her; she was utterly alone in this.

The Vampire deposited her into the back seat, where a grate prevented her from attacking him while he drove, and the doors could only be opened from the outside. Screaming in fury, she tried to kick out a window, kick down the divider, anything to secure her escape. She was a small woman but took pride in keeping her body strong. But with her recent blood loss, and all the Yoga in the world wasn't going to help her break out of a cop car.

"Eleanora, if you don't calm down and shut the Hel up, I will be forced to subdue you. And it will be painful. Do you understand?" he yelled over her screaming, addressing her as though she were a toddler in the throes of a temper tantrum instead of a traumatized murder witness and kidnap victim.

Did he really expect her to come along quietly?

"You killed that cop!" She flung the accusation at him, her words barely discernible to her own ears through the scream accompanying them.

"Yes, and your friends as well, and many others before them," he stated calmly as he glanced at her in the rearview mirror, his expression tight. "And I have allowed you to live."

The calm was the most unsettling part of his admission, solidifying he was without remorse. It was like watching a serial killer come to life in a TV crime drama.

"Perhaps now you will understand what I am capable of," he said, glancing up at her in the mirror, his eyes a swirling tempest of emotions. The words came out cold and unyielding, but the turmoil in his gaze didn't match the cruelty of his words.

Swallowing the remainder of her words down, Nora forced herself to look away from his haunted eyes. She didn't like that she saw remorse there. If he felt remorse, that meant there was part of him which was more human than monster.

The night sky emblazoned orange drew her attention, turning her in her seat to catch a glimpse of a raging inferno behind them. Flames licked high above the structure, their light blinding in the darkness of the night. Frowning, Nora realized she recognized the surrounding buildings, even in the warped illumination. "Is that the manor?" she asked, aghast.

"Yes," the Vampire replied flatly, his gaze straight ahead.

"Did you—"

"Yes," he interrupted.

Tears pricked the back of Nora's eyes as she thought about Tom, Judy, and Professor Hoffman lying on the ground inside the structure. "You're a monster," she whispered, swallowing to keep her tears from falling.

Cocking his head to the side, the Vampire studied her in the mirror. "It is a funeral pyre befitting a king," he replied.

"Yeah, but they wouldn't be there if you hadn't—" A sob choked off the last of her sentence.

"An unfortunate development," he conceded with a contrite nod.

"Unfortunate?" Nora shrieked. "They're *dead* because of you."

"I have made no secret of my monstrosities."

"You want me to hate you," Nora concluded, wiping at the stream of tears down her cheeks. "Does that make this easier for you?"

Silence descended over the vehicle for a few moments.

"No," he said with a sigh. "But your hate will protect you."

"From what?" she scoffed.

"Me."

Nora glanced up in the mirror, meeting his gaze. Forlorn was the only way she could describe his expression. "What do you mean?" she whispered, fear tinting her words.

"I have been apart from any semblance of civilization for nearly a century. Niceties are learned, groomed. When they are absent, instinct prevails."

"It's all instinct. You can't control yourself," Nora concluded with a gasp.

Slowly, he nodded his head in the mirror, his eyes never leaving hers.

Terror gripped Nora when she considered the implications of what he was saying. If he couldn't control himself from killing, there was nothing preventing him from snapping and taking her life.

"Except when you are near," he added.

"What?" Nora's voice trembled as her gaze snapped back up to his. "But—"

"I cannot explain it," he admitted. "I am able to retain a shred of control when you are near."

"That's why you're keeping me alive?" she balked.

"Part of it."

"And what's the other part?" she asked, truly terrified for the answer.

He pursed his lips but did not reply.

Turning from his image in the mirror, she stared into the darkness outside the window, unable to see any shapes and having no idea what direction, they were headed. "Where are we going?" she asked, keeping her eyes glued to the inky expanse beyond the glass.

"Paris," he answered, both surprising her at the answer and the fact that he actually told her.

"Are we driving the whole way there?" she asked, surprised he'd essentially taken the scenic route.

"Of course, unless you know a faster way."

"We could take the train," she offered, keeping as much of the hopeful note from her voice and expression from her face as she could. Although traveling in a police car might attract some attention, there wasn't much of a chance for escape from the back of a secure car. Even if they got pulled over by another officer, the chances the Vampire would just kill that officer were pretty high. At least with the train, they would be in a public place and her chances to get away from him increased substantially.

The Vampire scoffed at her and gave a knowing look in the mirror.

Was she really so transparent?

"It's faster than driving," she told him, going for nonchalance.

Studying her face in the mirror, he seemed to mull over the possibility. "If you give your word you will not attempt to escape, we will take the train."

Busted.

Nora's hope plummeted. Apparently she *was* that transparent.

"People will get hurt if I have to come after you," he warned.

The dangerous edge to his voice reminded her she was still his captive.

"I give my word," she mumbled, scowling.

Great, now there would be even more people in danger, and she was no closer to escape.

CHAPTER ELEVEN

"Can I ask you a question?" Nora requested, inwardly rolling her eyes at herself.

"Was that not a question? And no," he denied, raising an eyebrow at her without his gaze ever leaving the screen of her phone.

He had commandeered her phone as soon as he closed the door to their private car in the train. When she had told him it was a phone, he laughed and told her he was alive for the advent of the phone, and this was so much more. He had demanded she show him how to use it. She showed him how to dial a call and how to search the internet. After she'd demonstrated how he could look up almost anything on the internet—by typing 'Vampire' into the search function—he'd snatched the phone back from her and hadn't relinquished it since, not allowing her to see what he was searching.

"What's your name?"

Glancing up at her, he raised an eyebrow, but didn't answer.

An intensity she hadn't seen on the car ride had settled over him, along with a cold, hard glint to his eyes she liked even less than the tumultuous emotions indicating his level of instability. Every word out of his mouth since stepping aboard the train had been edged with cruelty.

"I mean, what should I call you? I can't just call you 'Vampire,'" she pressed.

"You may call me Master," he said with a smirk.

Nora's mouth snapped shut. No way, was she going to call him Master.

"Are you opposed to the title?" he queried, glancing up at her from beneath his eyebrows, his eyes narrowed menacingly.

"I—uh," Nora stuttered, then swallowed hard. "No." It was strange for her to think she would much prefer to be speaking with the Vampire from the car ride. This version was cold and calculating.

"Good. I am called Endre. Any other questions?"

Nora guessed he wasn't *really* offering for her to ask additional questions, but maybe some conversation would dull the edges and relieve the tension she could plainly see straining the breadth of his shoulders. He was anxious. She didn't know what exactly was making him feel anxious, but he was clearly not thrilled with being on this train. "How long were you buried there?" she pried, watching his lightning-quick fingers race across the screen.

It seemed everything he did was done a fraction of a step ahead of her. When they had entered the train station in the pitch black of night, he had taken both pieces of luggage in one hand and kept a firm grip on her arm with the other. If she moved a half a step too far from him in any direction, she was met with excruciating pain. When she contemplated screaming for help, all he had to do was give her a look which reminded her of her promise and the pain he would rain down upon every innocent bystander if she made a move against him. To protect those around her, oblivious to the kinds of creatures stalking the night right next to them, she allowed him to herd her to the ticket counter and then to the train like a docile, little lamb.

There was hope, though. They used her credit card to purchase the train tickets. Credit cards meant electronic information trails, breadcrumbs for some hope of rescue to follow. Flashes of the police officer lying on the floor of the villa assaulted her memory, sending a shudder through her. Endre was able to best him, but she had to hope he wouldn't be able to withstand the force of many of them. God, she hoped if they came, they brought an army. Either that or she signed the death warrant of anyone who apprehended them without some major fire power.

"Since 1923," The Vampire answered her nearly-forgotten question, not meeting her gaze.

Nora let her eyes wander over him and admonished herself for the warmth spreading through her when she gazed at him. *Biology*, she reminded herself. The pull toward him wasn't as strong as even a few hours ago, but she didn't know how all of these pheromones worked. Maybe they were stronger after she had his blood and waned over time. Or maybe she was building up some kind of tolerance. Or maybe he wasn't using them anymore because he found his threats were enough to gain her compliance without resorting to sexual warfare. Imagery of him without a scrap of clothing popped into her head, and she mentally shook herself to chase them away.

"If you're a... How can you be out in the sunlight? Do you have a magic ring or something? You don't sparkle or anything," she prattled in an attempt to push visions of his glorious naked body from her mind. She had to admit she was both curious about how Vampire life worked, and desperate to find a weakness, considering he exploited her humanity every chance he got.

His eyes flicked up to meet hers.

Now the familiar clenching in her core accompanying his gaze came back in full force. He had to be controlling her hormones somehow. It wasn't her, right? Maybe the pheromones were stronger when he looked at her. Nora fought valiantly against the arousal and the hormones flooding her system like a tsunami, and then ebbed as she stared into his blue depths. There was something in those eyes which drew her in. She'd heard it said eyes are the window to the soul, but she never really believed until gazing into his. She wouldn't pretend she could interpret the mysteries hidden behind his façade, but his eyes spoke of pain and suffering, of sadness.

The intensity of his stare was too much and Nora adjusted her focus to the alluring shape of his mouth, which brought an onslaught of blood to her nether regions. In hindsight, it may have been as dangerous as holding his gaze. All her thoughts turned to their encounter in the ruined manor, with his lips so near to touching hers. Then his words came rushing back to her, 'I do not play with my food.' *Food.* She was nothing to him but bodily nourishment. The reminder sobered her instantly.

Endre stared at her without comment.

So, she thought for a moment that he wouldn't answer.

"Rings? Sparkles? What are you on about?" he demanded, brows knit together in confusion.

"I'm running through my mental catalog of pop culture Vampire lore," she ruminated, glancing quickly to ensure the door was closed, since she uttered the V-word aloud.

"I have noticed," Endre scoffed, gesturing to the phone in his hand, "Modern humans seem to have some... interest in my kind. More so than they ever have had in the past. Throughout human history, legends of Vampires have drifted in and out of the oral traditions of cultures. Mostly used as cautionary tales against roaming the night and lying with strange men." His eyes wandered over her body, heat filling his gaze. "But," he continued after clearing his throat, "most of those legends were forgotten, or regarded as superstitions and the ramblings of the insane and paranoid when I last walked the earth. We put a fair amount of effort into dismissing these legends as myths. However, it seems your generation has resurrected stories of Vampires and spun them into gold. The idea of us being fodder for books and dreams come to life as forms of entertainment, you regard my kind with some sort of romantic fascination."

"If the stories are all wrong, why don't your people set the record straight? Use your influence to erase the romanticism?"

"If you were a predator, little lamb, would you want your prey to fear you? Or would you exploit their curiosity, knowing it would make your existence easier when they no longer enact safeguards to protect against your kind?" He tilted his head, watching her curiously.

Unsure if he expected her to answer, Nora remained silent.

"What *is* the fascination with Vampires which captivates you so?" With his brow furrowed, he continued to study her.

"I suppose it's the idea of living forever. Life seems so short as a human, we've barely begun living it before it's over. Why wouldn't we choose to seek out immortality?"

"Make no mistake, Eleanora, being a Vampire is not a life to be celebrated. Any who share this fate deserves your fear and pity alike. It is a lonely existence, filled with untold violence and copious bloodshed. This second 'life', if it can even truly be called that, is not to be revered, but rather, reviled." The

Vampire shook his head, his expression filled with sorrow.

"Would you give it up to be human again?" she asked, watching him closely while waiting for his answer.

"You have no idea." Shaking his head, he scoffed at the ceiling, then met her curious gaze.

"Why? I mean, I can see wanting to be rid of drinking blood, but to give up an unending life? Think of all the things you could do." Nora leaned forward in her seat.

"I have done plenty. You do not know what it means to watch the world age and decay before your eyes. To see all those you love wither in old age and fall victim to death. You want this? A life of death and destruction, merely so you could live to watch the world reduced to dust?"

Breath caught in her throat, she stared at him mutely. Was he asking her what she thought he was asking her? "I don't know," she whispered, shaking her head. "If it's so horrible, why continue on at all?"

"Are you suggesting I willingly end my second life? Or are you offering to do it for me?" He raised his eyebrows in challenge.

"No… maybe. I'm just wondering what would make such a life worth living for centuries on end if it's how you describe it. There has to be a reason for you to keep enduring, right?"

"I have my reasons."

"Can you die?" Nora perched on the edge of her seat, captivated by the discussion. Over the last several hours, he had been closed off and spoke in riddles when prompted to reveal more about *anything*. Now, she might at least learn of some way she could defend herself.

A frown turned down the corners of his mouth, not pleased with the direction the conversation had turned. "I will tell you this… I have lived longer than you can imagine, and you have borne witness to the healing capabilities of my blood. I am not easy to kill. So, if you seek to find a weakness of mine to exploit, you will find none. You are bound to me now and your mortality looms on the horizon. When you have outlasted your usefulness, then, and only then, will I dispatch you myself," he stated nonchalantly with a shrug, but while his words said one thing, the haunted sheen of his eyes said another.

"Why do you keep antagonizing me like that?" she whispered, her gaze directed to the floor.

"I do not know what you mean."

"You know exactly what I mean," she said, directing her glower to those intense blue eyes. "Why do you insist on reminding me you're going to kill me?"

"I continue to remind you, and yet you seem to not fear it. Can you already feel how shortened your life is?" the Vampire asked, a crease between his brows, as if he was genuinely curious.

Nora let out a snort. His nonchalance in regard to ending her life chilled her, but there was something in the way he continued to reiterate his intent that planted a seed of doubt. It was as if his bravado was more for his benefit that her own. He already told her he needed her, but the question was for how long. By the way he spoke to her, he didn't know.

"Or have you gotten it into your pretty head that I intend to transform you into a being like me?" Cocking his head to the side, he studied her, searching for the answer in her expression as much as her words.

"No," Nora whispered, the single word quaking in conjunction with the tremble of her body. Had she ever thought she would emerge from this nightmare alive? Or with any semblance of life?

"I would spare you that Hel. And yet, to die so young..." Endre brushed his hand along the stubble at his chin, seemingly deep in thought. "You die in any scenario." His gaze swung to her, his expression pained, his eyes full of sorrow.

"What does that mean?" she whispered, fighting her instinct to flee. Did he intend to kill her now? Had she already outlasted her usefulness?

"You do not know, do you?" He examined her expression closely, his eyes narrowed in suspicion.

"Know what?" Nora swallowed thickly, fighting back the impending sense of condemnation. The battle was futile, because with no way to escape the Vampire, she truly was doomed.

"Maybe it is just as well that you remain ignorant. Your death by my hand will prove more merciful than the fate awaiting you otherwise." With a deep sigh, his gaze dropped to the phone still clutched in his hand. "I could change that fate," he whispered.

Nora wasn't sure the words were meant for her. "How?" she asked, a modicum of hope taking root in her chest at the notion he might take pity on her and release her once he no longer needed her.

His gaze snapped up to her, surprised, as if realizing he spoke the words aloud. Quickly, his expression morphed to cold indifference. "You are a curious little pet," he mocked with a chuckle, emphasizing his perceived 'ownership' of her. He glanced down at the time on her phone, then back up to her. "There are yet several hours before we arrive at our destination. Your questions amuse me and pass the time, so I will allow them. What other queries do you have, *pet*?"

The softness in his tone gave Nora the impression he used the word 'pet' as an endearment. Would she ever prove to be endearing enough to spare her life? For a moment, she almost decided to remain silent and refuse to entertain him. But the more she considered the plan, the more she realized he was presenting her with a golden opportunity to learn more about him and Vampires in general. The information he might share may prove to be useful in saving her life.

"You never answered my question about daylight," Nora said, tilting her head in a caricature of curiosity.

Endre frowned a little but seemed to mull over the answer to her question, nonetheless. "Are you familiar with the anatomy of the human eye, Eleanora?" he quizzed.

Nora furrowed her brow, attempting to recall not only the lessons she learned in school on human anatomy, but also piecing together why such knowledge was relevant to their current conversation. "Uh, I think so. Rods and cones, irises and pupils and all that, why?"

Giving a tsk, he continued, "Vampire eyes differ from human eyes. They are closer to the structure of nocturnal animals. We have pupils which open wide and cover the entire front of the eye. We also develop a glowing layer of the eye, similar to what you see in a wolf or cat's eyes when a light is shone on them at night. Unlike most nocturnal animals, however, we still see in color and in very fine detail in the dark."

"Okay, so you can see in the dark…" Nora led, unclear as to the connection to her original question.

"Vampires' eyes, not our skin, are sensitive to sunlight. Your modern lore assumes the reason my kind avoids the sun is because of skin sensitivity. We can handle sunlight fine, in smaller doses and usually accompanied by a slight headache if we do not have eye protection."

"A headache?" Nora challenged skeptically, her eyebrows raised.

"Yes, similar to when a human has a migraine and is sensitive to light, the headache gets worse. But our remedy is much different," he explained, showing her his fangs, insinuating blood was the old-fashioned Vampire cure for a migraine.

Nora shuddered at the thought. Her discomfort, however, wasn't enough to quell her curiosity, especially when he was so willing to divulge the information. "Okay, what about the fangs? How do they work?"

"I would think that one was obvious. Sharp bone puncturing soft skin," he stated, setting aside the phone. Leaning forward, he rested his elbows on his knees, clasping his hands together as he grinned playfully.

That grin was devastatingly handsome. If she hadn't already been his captive, that was the only bait he would have needed to lure her in. He appeared as though he was enjoying the conversation, maybe even a little excited to share his knowledge.

"I get you pierce the skin, but are they like snake fangs, or what?" she queried, leaning toward him to get a closer look at his fangs. Apparently, she had a macabre curiosity about the things which almost killed her—and may kill her yet.

"Or what?" he asked with a chuckle, apparently amused at the vernacular. "Yes and no. Snakes have hollow fangs which inject venom into their victims from a gland. It is a one-way avenue and they do not generally feed on blood. However, Vampires do have similarly hollow fangs. Each has a hole in the back at the gum line, so we can use them like straws to siphon blood. And we do not administer venom to our victims," Endre educated, opening his mouth up wider to give her a good look.

"Are they out all the time? Do you cut yourself on them?" Nora investigated, tilting her head to get a better look.

"No, that would be much too conspicuous. And we have evolved in the ways to remain as *unnoticeable* as possible. Our fangs are retractable. They extend when needed and retract to avoid injury to ourselves."

"Concealed weapons," Nora mumbled as she pulled farther away from his mouth. "Speaking of weapons… what about garlic and holy water and wooden stakes?"

"What about them? Trying to find ways to kill me again?" he questioned with an arrogant smirk.

Nora shrugged and gave him a dazzling smile.

His smirk dropped from his face quickly.

Nora was suddenly terrified she had taken her interrogation too far.

"Holy water does not do a thing. We would all have to believe in the same holy things for that to work. Garlic does nothing to deter us. And wooden stakes, well, they fucking hurt when you get stabbed by them, but they do not kill us directly unless appropriately positioned," he replied seriously.

Nora almost snorted. He'd threatened her life and killed others in his wake, but his speech always seemed to be eloquent and well-articulated, so hearing the word 'fuck' from him was jarring. "Okay, what about having to be invited inside?" she questioned, leaning back with her arms crossed to ward off the sudden chill she got thinking about how little she really knew about these monsters.

"We go where we please, invited or not," he said with a shrug. Giving her a genuine smile, he encouraged her to continue the interrogation, "What else, Eleanora? I can see more questions teeming in that brain of yours."

"Reflections in mirrors and photographs?" she pressed, assuming he would know what she meant. She'd seen his reflection many times, but was interested in where the lore came from. There had to be a kernel of truth in the myth.

"I can see my reflection just fine," he deadpanned, gesturing to the window where Nora, too, could see his reflection. "As for photographs, it is less that we do not show up and more that we do not *want* to. It would not do to be documented in photographs and be alive then still look the same as the day it was taken. And the flash for a photograph would give us away. Remember what I told you about eye structure? A photograph would show that reflective layer humans do not have. The medical term for that layer is tapetum," he said, absently turning her phone over in his hand.

"Doctor Vampire," Nora laughed at the ridiculous notion.

He gave her a strange look and then that dazzling grin again. "You are a curious one. I have heard tell curiosity killed the cat," he jested with a glint in his eyes.

Nora shrugged. "Well, I guess it's a good thing I'm not a cat. And I guess I do have a morbid curiosity. I like to know how this all works. This is an opportunity to ask questions I never thought I'd have. Like my own version of *Interview With A Vampire*. I've grown up on stories and movies about Vampires, and all the tales have varying components with regards to anatomy and weapons. And wars with werewolves or other mythological creatures. Are there werewolves?"

"No, no werewolves that I know of." He shook his head.

Nora got the impression his answer wasn't the entire truth.

"What about other mythical creatures, like dragons and fairies and stuff like that?" Nora demanded.

"*Nei*. Eleanora, you have to realize Vampires are more of a mutation of the human species than mythical beings. There are some aspects of our nature and existence we are still unable to explain with science, but we are performing research to unlock those mysteries, as humans have done for thousands of years to understand their own biology," he said, leaning back in his seat and regarding her curiously. "I think you have asked enough questions. Time for some of my own."

"Okay..." Nora answered warily, sinking further into her seat, not a fan of the idea of letting him dig deeper into her life. He had invaded enough already.

Endre regarded her casually, and then leaned forward so he was only a foot away. "You are a university student, yes?"

"Yes."

"Studying archaeology, I assume?"

"Yes." Short and to the point, she didn't want to give him any more ammunition to use against her.

"What year are you in at the university?"

"This internship was my final course for credit. I could graduate any time now," Nora contemplated sadly. She thought how walking across a stage in front of strangers frightened the crap out of her, but she wouldn't get to do it now.

If he noticed her discomfort, he said nothing about it. "How old are you?"

"I just turned twenty-two."

"Who is this?" he interrogated, showing her a picture on her phone of her and John from a year or so ago, right before they broke up. "Is this your lover?" he demanded, a hint of jealousy in his words.

"That's my ex-boyfriend John. No, he's not my lover. And I don't really want to talk about him," Nora explained, dropping her gaze to her hands in her lap. It still surprised her that the subject of her failed relationship was still raw, even after a year. She had always thought she was stronger than that.

"Come now, Eleanora, you wanted to play this game of questions. I answered yours, it is only fair you answer mine," he cajoled.

"I did, I answered your questions," Nora snapped, foolishly daring him to contradict her with semantics.

"Ah, it ended in heartbreak then. It is seldom that relationships do not. Better to have loved and lost, than to have never loved at all, some say. A pity love lost is all you will ever know. You are so young. I am doing you a favor, really by killing you before you know real devastating heartbreak. Despite your human fairytales of love and undying devotion altering us creatures of the night into living against our nature, true love does not exist for either human or Vampire. Alas, I believe our game has taken a downturn," he remarked bitterly, his expression sour. "Though I speak truth, my views are not always well received."

Nora stared at him in disbelief. His words cut her to the bone and left her raw. She didn't know why she allowed his lecture to affect her so potently, it wasn't as though some of the things he said weren't words she'd told herself a million times after parting ways with John.

"Find a hotel in Paris, near the river," Endre directed suddenly, tossing the phone to her. "Do not communicate with anyone. I believe you understand the stakes if you do."

She did. Those stakes seemed to involve one common factor—death. Whether it was hers or someone else's was difficult to say. Nora stared down at the phone in her hands. The little envelope icon had appeared, indicating a message waiting. It took all of her willpower not to open the email. It would be so easy to shoot a message off to someone. And then what? What would she write? That she'd been kidnapped by a Vampire? That would sound ridiculous. And who would she send it to? She didn't know anyone in Italy, let alone Paris where they were going. Maybe she could send an email to Giana or Dave. But that would only get them and her, killed.

"Eleanora, your hesitation does not inspire much confidence in your abilities to follow direction," the Vampire across from her insinuated unhappily.

The sound of his voice startled her from her thoughts of sending out an S.O.S., so Nora quickly opened her browser and began searching hotels.

CHAPTER TWELVE

Endre watched the woman intently as her fingers moved across the screen of her phone. The device was certainly something to behold, with the world's information at his fingertips. He had spent the beginning of their train ride exploring what Eleanora explained was the internet. After he had satisfied his curiosity with modern tales of Vampires to ensure they still remained musings of fiction and ravings of the paranoid, rather than exposure of reality, he had searched for any clues which might lead him to the whereabouts of Lorenzo. Endre had set them on the path to Paris, suspecting Lorenzo would reside in his home city, instead of staying in Italy. He had mentioned several times when they were still friends that he detested Italy and longed for the civility of Paris. Endre's searches proved to be fruitless; he supposed he would have to get information on Lorenzo's whereabouts the old fashioned way by torturing it out of Lorenzo's minions when he arrived in France.

Interestingly enough, it was not the drive to find Lorenzo which occupied Endre's thoughts. It was the woman across from him. Before him was an impossible choice. He was beginning to grow fond of Eleanora, her passion for life and her curiosity about the world around her inspired him. She was certainly brighter than he would have given her credit for at first glance. And yet, hers was a light which would ultimately be snuffed out much too soon. Either the disease ravaging her body would claim her life, or he would.

But that was not the decision to be made.

The choice would be if he could bear to lose such a bright light from this world when he removed her from it, sending her to the afterlife. Or, if he should drag her brilliance into the mire of the dark world he resided in, risking extinguishing it altogether?

CHAPTER THIRTEEN

Outside the entrance to the Paris hotel, Endre gripped Nora's arm tightly and whispered low into her ear, his voice strained, "I trust I do not have to reiterate the pain which awaits, should you attempt to alert anyone here to what I am and your current... situation? If you *do* attempt to sound an alarm, I will put a swift end to them, and then you. Their blood will be a black mark on your soul when I deliver you to the afterlife."

The tension in his body she noticed during the train was still there, pulling his body so taut, she worried he would snap at any moment. Nora nodded quickly, and the grip on her arm loosened slightly. Undoubtedly, she would find bruises when she looked later.

Upon steering them to the front desk, the Vampire addressed the clerk in flawless French.

How many languages did the man speak? How many places had he lived in the shadows over the centuries, how many lifetimes had he drifted in and out of? His voice snapped her back to the hotel lobby where both the clerk and her warden stared at her expectantly.

The clerk appeared confused and concerned.

Endre was clearly annoyed. "The payment, Eleanora, my dear," he addressed her with saccharine in his tone.

"Oh, of course. Sorry, I mean *pardon*. I'm so exhausted, I didn't sleep a wink on the train," Nora rambled as she fumbled through the contents of her wallet for her credit card. Glancing quickly at Endre, she hoped he didn't have a great enough understanding of how the plastic money worked and how those transactions could be traced back to them. Using her card might be the one thing to save her. If authorities were monitoring her accounts, and she could imagine they would after finding a dead officer in the villa she was staying at, they would come here looking for her. Leaving a trail of electronic transactions for them to follow was the closest she would come to dropping breadcrumbs for them.

"Of course, *Madame*," the clerk responded with an apologetic smile when she took the card.

The clerk swiped the card and typed into the computer before handing the card back to Nora and then handing the room keys to Endre while rattling off some directions or instructions in French.

Endre frowned slightly at the plastic rectangles in his hand as he turned them over, clearly expecting an actual *key* to open their room door.

"*Madame, Monsieur,* enjoy your stay," the clerk concluded in English, for Nora's benefit, Nora assumed.

Endre led Nora to the elevators with a hand at the small of her back. To anyone else, the placement of his hand would look intimate, but to her, it held a warning. The lives of innocents were in her hands. A tingle ran through her at his touch, as did a surprising streak of jealousy when she wondered if he'd used his infamous pheromones on the desk clerk.

Surprising, indeed.

Nora stood in the middle of the hotel room with her arms crossed, attempting to calm the shaking of her limbs. She didn't know what she was supposed to do now. There had still been no information from Endre on what exactly they were doing here. He continued to remind her she wasn't privy to his plans, citing the rationale that the more she knew, the more danger she was in.

Frankly, she was having a difficult time coming up with a scenario in which she would be in *more* danger than she was currently in. A glance to the door brought plots of escape to her mind. There was no way she was fast enough to outrun him, but even that knowledge didn't prevent her from considering it.

"Come here, Eleanora," Endre beckoned from a chair in the corner where he'd collapsed upon dumping their luggage in the corner. Much of the tension in his body had dissipated the moment he stepped through the door to their room.

"Nora," she corrected.

"Nora, come here," he ordered, his tone soft and coaxing.

Nora slowly moved forward until she stood in front of him.

Reaching out to her, he took her hand, his grip gentle, his fingers soft against her skin.

Her breath caught in her throat as he ran his fingers over her wrist, carefully pulling her toward him.

"I apologize, I need to feed," he explained, pulling her to stand between his knees. "It would be more comfortable for you to kneel."

Panic and dread took over her system, his grip on her wrist tightening as she instinctively moved to flee. In the back of her mind she knew if he didn't feed from her, it would be from someone else – and although the thought that another person might not survive crossed her mind – she wasn't selfless enough to drop to her knees and comply with his wishes. After all, she might die during this feeding if he failed to keep a grip on his control.

"Nora," he warned an edge of command in his voice. "The more you struggle, the more painful it will be. Comply now, and I give you my word to be as gentle as possible."

Resistance still held her firm. How could she willingly put herself in a position where pain and blood loss were her only options?

"I do not want to have to use violence to force your compliance, but I will if you leave me no choice," he reminded.

"And I'm just supposed to accept that?"

"I expect your sense of self-preservation will be accepting when faced with the alternative."

Death.

The pressure on her wrist bordered on painful as he steadily pulled her toward the floor. A whimper escaped her amidst the turmoil in her mind—give in, and live for some indeterminate amount of time, or stand her ground and die?

"My patience is wearing thin," he warned, the tenderness that was in his voice earlier all but gone.

Nora dropped to her knees in defeat, hanging her head, studying the pattern of the carpet through watery eyes.

"Much better," Endre praised, placing his fingers beneath her chin and tilting her head to expose her neck. Scooting forward on the chair, he bent to reach her.

The alluring scent of him wafted over Nora with his movement, replacing the trembling of her body from fear with anticipation. Closing her eyes, she waited.

Soft lips brushed the sensitive skin on her neck, skimming along the line of her jaw. Pulling in tiny breaths, Nora grew light-headed. When Endre's mouth pressed lightly to hers, she let out a small moan. But then the delicious feel of his mouth on hers was gone, replaced with a sharp pricking pain radiating from her neck, stealing her breath away when she opened her mouth to cry out. Nausea rolled through her with the sensation of the Vampire sucking the blood from her body.

Endre moaned deeply as he pulled in mouthful after mouthful. His hands gripped her desperately, one wrapped around her neck to keep her head in place, the other around her waist, pulling her into his form. Faster he drank, his manner morphing from gentle to feral.

Placing her hand on his chest, she attempted to push him away, but his grip grew tighter and more possessive, his feeding more insistent. Black edged into her vision, and the ocean began to roar in her ears. "Stop," she gasped around the grip at her throat.

With a growl, Endre unlatched from her neck, his grip on Nora disappearing as though she were made of molten metal.

Dizziness overwhelmed her and she crumbled to a heap at his feet, though at least she could breathe again.

"Godsdammit," he cursed, his voice sounding far away from where Nora lay on the floor. "Nora," he coaxed as he lifted her body from the floor.

Her eyelids were like lead, and no matter how hard she tried, she couldn't lift them.

"Nora?" Endre called again, his voice sounding as though the ocean in her ears had taken him under its waves. "Stay with me," he pled.

Then the world went black and silent.

CHAPTER FOURTEEN

"Godsdammit," Endre growled to the silent hotel room as he arranged Nora's unconscious form on the bed. He should have known better. He should have known his self-control would be tested when drinking from her again. It had been far too long since he had been required to display restraint, he had no idea what went through his mind. It did not help that the taste of her blood was one of the sweetest he had ever had, making it that much harder to stop without draining her dry. Even now, as resolute as he was to save her, his body still pushed him toward finishing his meal.

It was imperative he leave this place and hunt among Paris' underbelly tonight before body overrode mind and drove him to action he would regret the moment his bloodlust subsided. But first, Nora needed *his* blood. Then, and only then, would he leave her to fulfill his darkest need to glut himself on criminals and vagrants.

Opening his mouth wide, he slashed a fang across his trembling wrist. There was no way in this world or the next he would to allow her to die tonight, especially not by his hand. As much as he disliked admitting it, he was growing fond of the woman. Most disturbing, though, were the feelings growing *beyond* mere fondness.

Tilting her head back, Endre lifted Nora's lips apart and watched the crimson flow from his wrist fill her mouth. A smirk played at the corners of his mouth when he thought about how much easier this was to feed her when she was not fighting him. Her fight was one of the things he had come to admire about her. In his long life, it had been difficult to find a woman who could compete with the courage of the shield maidens he fought side-by-side with in his first life. Until Nora. There was no doubt in his mind she belonged among the Valkyries.

When the wound at his wrist healed, he collapsed into the same chair where he almost claimed her life. With relief, he watched the deep rise and fall of her chest as she breathed, and listened to the steady beat of her heart. Tonight could have ended in tragedy. It still could if he did not leave to feed elsewhere. If he were going to sustain them both from his blood, her body requiring a significant amount to keep her illness at bay, he would need to claim several victims tonight. He harbored no illusion that he would be able to restrain himself from taking the lives of his victims, yet that was why he would hunt in the gutters so he would not feel the crushing guilt of claiming the innocent.

Striding to the window, Endre drew back the curtains and surveyed the empty alleyway three floors below. Darkness shrouded the narrow corridor, providing the perfect cover for a creature of the night to slip away unnoticed. He glanced back at Nora's figure on the bed and pushed away his guilt. There was no place for guilt in his hunt for blood or his mission to locate Lorenzo. Yet, he felt remorse. Not only had he injured her, but by feeding her so much of his blood, he subjected her to the gruesome memories of his past through his blood memories—memories carried by the blood from one host to another, displaying scenes where the host has either had their blood spilled or spilled the blood of another. So many of his were brutal, and there was no way to control what she would see.

Leaning against the window, he closed his eyes and pushed back against the onslaught of blood memories of her life. As much as he would like to learn more about her, now was not the time. Though Nora did not have the capability to control the memories, after centuries of practice, he could. Snippets of her life pushed against his block, but he forced them back. He would much rather learn about her life from her than from his assault on her.

With one last look back at Nora's limp form and a deep breath, Endre dropped from the window into the alleyway below.

It did not take long before he encountered his first victim of the night. A dark figure huddled over a body a few streets from the hotel. The unmistakable noise of blood being siphoned from the Vampire's meal assaulted Endre's sensitive hearing. Such a grotesque sound. He was nearly upon the other Vampire, relying on his skills in the art of stealth from his previous life as a raiding warrior, before the creature's attention was drawn from the body at his feet to Endre's approach.

In a flash of movement, Endre had the Vampire by the throat, slamming his back against the stone wall of the building. It was not worth the effort to even spare a glance for the Vampire's meal, the heartbeat had ceased, there would be no saving that one.

"Where is Lorenzo?" Endre demanded in French, loosening his grip on the other Vampire's throat to allow him to respond. He did not recognize the Vampire, but that did not mean he was not some new batch of cronies turned by his old friend.

"Who the fuck are you?" his adversary challenged, a sneer pulling at his upper lip.

"Endre."

"Never heard of you," the Vampire replied with a chuckle. "Which means you have no power here. Fuck off."

"If you refuse to answer, I will end you," Endre warned, not wanting to dispatch a potential informant before he had been given ample opportunity to provide intel.

The Vampire let out a strangled laugh. "If you kill me, he'll come for you."

"I am counting on it."

"You'll have to kill me before I tell you a thing," the Vampire's tone was filled with defiance and bravado, but there was real fear in his eyes. Whether it was from Endre's threat, or what fate would befall him should he reveal Lorenzo's secrets, Endre did not know.

"That settles that then." Pulling a short dagger from within the folds of the Vampire's coat, Endre thrust it through the creature's ribcage, ramming it into his heart.

His victim's eyes grew wide a moment before the light left them. Although this modern era preferred the use of firearms to blades, there was no quicker way to dispatch an enemy Vampire than piercing the heart. Lorenzo knew it, sending his men into the streets with hidden steel—just as he had done a century ago.

Opening his hand, Endre dropped the corpse to the ground, pulling the blade from the body on the way down. He had ventured into the night with no weapons of his own, counting on the expectation he would encounter a Vampire less experienced in combat than him and be able to relieve him of his weapons. He should have taken the police officer's firearm in Italy, but he had not been thinking clearly at the time. Searching the other Vampire's person, Endre removed the man's firearm, as well as a few other personal effects. Now, when he found another Vampire to interrogate, he would at least have a weapon to threaten them with, considering his name was not enough.

What he *should* have done was taken some of the Vampire's blood before he expired and sifted through his blood memories for information Lorenzo's whereabouts. He had been too hasty to dole out death, but next time he encountered one of his enemy's minions he would not be so merciful.

Glancing down at the body, he decided to leave it where it lay. He doubted it would take long for one of Lorenzo's men to discover it, and then they would be in pursuit of the killer. It was possible Endre could end his search here and wait for Lorenzo to find him.

Though that path may prove quicker, it was certainly more dangerous. His nemesis would have the element of surprise, as there was no telling how many of his horde would be sent to dole out justice. However, unless Endre left some kind of calling card on the body, Lorenzo would not know who it was he sought to pay for the crime. Then it would be Endre with the advantage of surprise.

After examining the position of the moon in the sky, he estimated he had very little time left before he needed to return to the hotel. Nora would awaken soon and he wanted to be there when she did. But before he could face her, he needed hunt so he would not be tempted to feed from her again.

It did not take long for Endre to find his meal. Two men provided a substantial dinner for him, deserving of their fate the moment they decided to mug a woman and pull her into a dark alley for sinister deeds. Fortunately for Endre, the woman was not conscious at the time he arrived and tore into his unsuspecting victims. He was also considerate enough to dispose of the bodies at the bottom of the river, so she would not have to witness the grisly scene he'd perpetrated. The men's blood was rank with the bitter palate of drugs, but at least the human scum he scraped from the gutters would stave off his bloodlust for a few more hours—keeping Nora safe from his thirst.

CHAPTER FIFTEEN

Steel clanging against steel sounded from all around Nora and the cries of men assaulted her ears. A battlefield. She was smack dab in the middle of a battle. When she attempted to raise her hands to clamp them over her ears, she discovered her limbs didn't move. A bearded man in furs brandishing a sword charged at her, and she was surprised to see a sword in her hand deflect the blow. She met each strike blow for blow until her sword swiped out and separated her opponent's head from his body. A scream welled up in her chest, but the only sound that came from her body was a grunt. It seemed no matter what Nora instructed her body to do—it wouldn't obey.

Her dream body moved with the lithe grace of a trained warrior—slashing, slicing and blocking with sword and shield, cutting down opponents as they appeared. The sight of so much blood turned her stomach. As her mind tried to block out the gore around her, a searing pain ripped through her abdomen and a guttural scream echoed inside her head. This time, her *hands did what she commanded. Her hand pressed into the wound now marring her and came away bloody.*

Nora was shocked to see the hands were that of a man. But more importantly, she was going to die. Before she gave in to the underworld, her sword sliced out at her assailant, giving him a quicker death than she would endure. Collapsing to her knees, she stared at the crimson liquid staining her fingers. She was going to die. The pain of remaining upright was too much to bear and she fell backward to stare at the bright blue expanse of the sky.

The battle raged on, not far from her—close enough she could still hear the clang of the metal and the screams of her dying brothers-at-arms, but far enough she didn't get trampled in the wake of the warriors who still fought. Soon, the sounds of fighting died out and there was only pain and the violent ringing in her ears. Then, only blackness. Blessed darkness.

A sound drew her from the blackness. Above her, a jet-black crow cawed as if calling to her, its cries echoing across the field. Her eyes focused and followed the flight of the bird as it droned on above her. Its call began to sound like words, leading her into her final moments of mortality. The encounter in her dream with the crow was eerily similar to her near-death experience in Italy.

This dream was so strange.

"Hel or Valhalla?" Nora's host whispered to the crow, or was it a raven?

"Neither, at least at the moment," a voice, raspy like sandpaper, answered from her right.

Nora rolled to the side to see if she was hallucinating in her last moments in the light. A man crouched beside her, tearing into the skin of his wrist with his abnormally sharp canines. The sight of the blood welling between his teeth nauseated her, but she could neither turn to vomit nor close her eyes to block out the image. The man brought his wrist to her lips and filled her mouth with his blood. She choked and sputtered but swallowed mouthfuls at a time just to keep breathing. The feeling of déjà vu held her on the edge of panic.

"Enough," the stranger whispered, pulling his hand away. Rising to his feet, he stared down at her, unmoving, as if waiting. A slow smile crept across his face when she was able to lift her hand. He reached down and pulled her to her feet.

Nora looked down and watched with morbid fascination as the skin and sinew of the wound began to pull itself together by fractions of an inch before her eyes. Her gaze snapped up to the stranger's face and noted the extraordinary beauty of him. She was in the presence of something not of this world.

A Vampire.

"Very good!" the man exclaimed with a warm chuckle. "You will do nicely," he declared, looking her up and down.

Nora surveyed the carnage around her. The battlefield was littered with the dead and the dying, and only moments before, she would have joined them in whatever afterlife was her lot. When she pried her eyes from the destruction of so much life lost, her eyes met with the stranger who'd saved her. His eyes were black pits, devoid of any warmth. Nora's borrowed body took a step backward, prepared to either fight or flee the monster before it. The demon's mouth turned up at the corners in a cruel facsimile of a smile, and faster than she could fathom, his hands reached up to her head and she heard the snap of her vertebrae before she was able to fully register her death.

Nora awoke with a strangled cry. "It wasn't real," she whispered to herself when the realization she was alive dawned on her.

"What did you dream?" a smooth, velvety voice inquired from the darkness.

Slapping her hand over her mouth, she stifled a whimper. Apparently, only part of her nightmares didn't exist in reality. In the dim light seeping from behind the curtains, she watched the Vampire's silhouette rise from the chair in the corner of the hotel room.

That's right. They were in Paris. She remembered now.

Nora tried to curl into the fetal position in the hopes of waking from *this* nightmare as well. A sharp pain in her abdomen stole her breath and sent a current through her body. She let out a shriek of pure agony when she could breathe again. Clutching at the pain, her fingertips were met with wetness. Her sobs bordered on hysteria when the bedside lamp clicked on, the light temporarily blinding her. And then all she saw was the red staining her hand.

"Shhhh…" he soothed, running his fingers over her hair.

The gesture was tender and sweet.

"What is it, Nora? What did you see?" Endre crooned into her ear.

She lifted her hand from her abdomen and stared with fear at the red coating it. It was just a dream. How could she be bleeding from a wound sustained in a dream?

CHAPTER SIXTEEN

Endre's eyes opened wide with surprise and he pushed Nora to her back to get a closer look at her wound. He lifted her blood-soaked shirt and stared at the gash marring her skin. Where had the injury come from?

When her sobs grew louder, he realized he gripped her too tightly. The sight and smell of her intoxicating blood nearly unhinged him, sending him to the dark place he did not wish to go. His logical brain trying to solve the riddle was at war with his instincts which screamed at him to tear into her flesh and extract every last drop of her essence before it was wasted. Logic somehow overrode primal hunger, and he moved quickly when his brain stuttered back to life, emerging from the cloud of bloodlust.

Picking her up, he whisked her to the bathtub, where he rinsed the laceration. He expected more of a protest from her until he took notice of her lethargy. Clearly, she had lost a lot of blood, although it did not appear to him as though there was enough blood on her clothes for as deep a wound as it was.

Quickly, he fed Nora some of his blood amidst her weak protests, smiling despite himself. Even in her current state, she was stubborn, displaying that spirit he admired. Lightly prodding the wound, he noted the infusion was stopping the bleeding. But without quite a bit more of his blood, she would need sutures. He considered his options; he had just fed from several humans, enough to spare more blood to heal her.

Frowning, he considered that the injury might be self-inflicted. The notion was far-fetched, and yet she bled from a wound deep enough to kill her—and *he* certainly had not given it to her.

With a sigh, Endre pushed away the enigma – for the moment – and opened his wrist again. There was no fight in her this time as he poured more of his life into her. As much as he disliked the idea of filling her with more Vampire blood, he needed her coherent to answer his questions. The origin of her wound was a mystery he needed to solve.

With a sense of detachment brought on by centuries of watching his blood work its magic, he observed her wound closing up by minuscule measures right before his eyes. A modern medical marvel. If only its magic extended to wiping the sickness from her body. But it was too late for that, the disease infiltrated the very marrow of her bones where the blood he craved was created. Even if he replaced every drop of her blood with his, her body would turn it against itself. There was only one possible outcome for her—death.

"Nora," he crooned in low tones meant to soothe her as much as himself while he struggled to push away thoughts of her impending death. "Where did this come from?" he prompted, running his finger along the now-sealed gash.

She winced, but opened her eyes. They were glassy and her voice drifted in from far away when she murmured, "My dream."

Endre frowned. "What dream? What else was in the dream?" he demanded. She was not exactly lucid, and maybe she had lost more blood than he had originally calculated.

As she described the dream with details he knew intimately from his own past, he grew angry with himself. Blood memories. How could he have overlooked the possibility? The reactions to blood memories were generally much milder, relying on one or two of the senses to replay the scene. There had only been a handful of times when he had experienced three different senses at a time, and never had he physically felt the pain of his victims in the way Nora had.

The memories themselves were enigmas, nothing he had ever been able to scientifically study. Over the centuries, however, it had become evident that volume of blood consumed correlated to the vividness of the memories. It would stand to reason then, that these especially intense experiences were a direct result of the overwhelming amount of his blood coursing through her body. He had given her far too much if she was waking with wounds which were his over a millennium ago.

Endre was running out of time. Nora's body continued to weaken despite the amount of blood he fed her. Glancing down at her, pain lanced through his chest as thoughts of her demise plagued him once more. Though he had threatened her with death early on in their journey to gain her obedience, knowing it was inevitable, the very idea of it turned his stomach now. To see her fierce spirit snuffed out would be a waste. There were two choices ahead of him, neither option ideal—did he allow her to die as the disease ravaged her body? Or did he alter her fate and condemn her to a life in the shadows by his side? The choice *should* have been simple, but it was not.

A shiver sent tremors through her form, her bottom lip quivering to remind him of the cool temperature of the water and the inevitable shock her body would surely experience after such a traumatic encounter with his blood memory.

Gathering her in his arms, Endre rose to his feet, a pink cascade of water falling from her body to join the pool of red in the tub.

Nora started as he lifted her into the air, her eyes flying open and those green depths spearing him with panic while she clutched at his body.

"Shhhh," he soothed, pulling a towel from the rack while he shifted her body to press against him, soaking his shirt. "We need go get you out of these wet clothes." His glance down at the way the wet fabric clung to her form was inevitable.

Her breasts were perfectly outlined and the darker hue of her nipples was barely visible through the sodden cotton, but it was enough to send the blood he had feasted on tonight flowing straight to his groin. Shivers wracked her body as he sat her on the toilet seat, her nipples peaking beneath her shirt in the chill air.

Endre managed to pry his eyes from her breasts, finding her gaze filled with terror. Was it his perusal of her body that terrified her so?

"I c-c-can do-o it," she stuttered through chattering teeth, her eyes wide as she watched him.

"Nora, you are very weak," he began to protest. He did not believe for one second with the way her body trembled she was capable of removing her clothing herself. Then again, perhaps it was his baser desires which pushed him to argue, wanting to be the one to undress her and drink in the splendor of her naked body. He should not want that. He should not want *her*, this human. This frail creature destined to die within weeks—with or without his intervention.

"Please," she whispered.

The plea within her gaze was so pitiful it served to sober him. With a nod, he turned his back, refusing to the leave the confines of the bathroom in the event she was too weak to perform the task herself. "Here." Reaching behind him, he offered her the towel he still gripped.

Movement sounded from behind him, and knowing she was laying herself bare just beyond his sight was enough to drive him mad. From behind him, Endre heard her let out a soft grunt, and her heart rate increased along with her breathing.

"I," she started, a sound akin to a sob breaking from her. "I n-need h-help," she stammered, her voice filled with defeat.

Drawing in a breath to calm the throbbing in his loins, Endre turned to her. Though it should not have been humorous, finding her arms stuck in the wet cloth of her shirt brought a fleeting grin to his face.

"I-I'm s-s-s-stuck." Her teeth clattered together as she pointed out the obvious.

"I am afraid you are," Endre remarked with a sigh, attempting to infuse his words with disinterest and annoyance. It did not work.

With efficient movements, he whisked the shirt from over her head, wishing he were not as affected by the sight of her as he was. His breath caught in his throat as his gaze wandered over her bare breasts, taking in the creamy white of her skin, pebbled from the cold and topped with dusky nipples drawn tight.

Even with the tremor of her limbs, Nora was quick to shield his view with her arms.

"It is nothing I have not seen before," he scoffed with practiced nonchalance, his fingers itching to touch her and betray the ruse. He had seen plenty of breasts in his centuries on this Earth, but somehow none seemed to compare to hers. It was then that a thought hit him— he was falling in love with his prey. "Impossible," he growled aloud.

Nora startled and drew back from the ferocity in his words. "What?" she whispered, her eyes wide as she took him in.

"Nothing," he snapped, irritation at his heart's choice of amour. "Here." Shoving a towel at the unsuspecting human, he turned his head away from the alluring view. In a way, everything made sense with this epiphany. Knowing she was dying *should* have encouraged him to provide her with mercy and end her suffering before it began, and yet he continued to feed her his blood with the false hope it would cure her of her disease. He knew it would not. But by continuing to infuse her body with his blood, he ensured one outcome and one only—she would become a Vampire.

By his estimate, Nora's body would only carry her through the world of the living for another week or two at most. Regardless of whether she died by his hand or by the disease, his blood would remain in her system and thereby facilitate her transformation to the in-between world he lived in as a Vampire.

Endre's stomach churned, but if he was not mistaken, it was with nervousness. How would she react to knowledge he had sealed her fate to his? Glancing back to her, he took in the ghostly pallor of her skin and the blue tinge to her lips, her entire countenance appearing undead already. It would be so easy, to break her neck right now and end her suffering.

"W-what?" his human asked, her eyes wide as she searched his expression, perhaps seeing his struggle play across his face. "Why are you l-looking at me l-like that?" she whispered, her heart rate erratic while she examined his face.

Inhaling deeply, Endre pushed away the metallic scent of her blood in the air and smoothed his expression. As much as the idea of making her a Vampire immediately appealed to him, perhaps it was best to converse with her on the matter first. "You require warmth and rest." Taking the towel from where she clutched it, he draped it over her chest. More reminders of her nudity were most unwelcome at the moment, but the knowledge was ever-present as he lifted her into his arms once again.

"My jeans are still wet," she protested as he stepped toward the bathroom exit.

Glancing down at Nora's denim-clad legs draped over his arm, Endre sighed with the confirmation. "So they are." Stooping, he set her feet to the floor. "Place your hands on my shoulders and I will remove them." Warm satisfaction coursed through him as she grappled for his shoulders to steady herself when he dropped to his knees before her, reaching for the button on her pants.

At Nora's sharp intake of breath, his gaze snapped to hers. Dark pupils expanded to cover the green of her irises. Her breath quickened when he held her stare as he popped open the button on her pants and dragged the zipper down. The sound of the metal teeth separating filled the silence of the small room, the only sound louder in Endre's ears was the rush of her quickening heartbeat.

With his eyes locked on hers, he peeled the soaked cloth over her hips, brushing his fingers along her chilled skin as he went. It was pure torture, undressing this woman for a purpose other than submitting to his most carnal desires.

"Lift your foot," he managed to croak out when he reached her ankles.

Nora complied shakily, her body swaying closer to him as she struggled to keep her balance.

Perhaps it would have been easier to undress her, had he laid her on the floor, but just the thought brought visions of pressing his body into hers against the cold tile. Stifling a groan, Endre repeated his actions with her other foot, tossing her jeans to the side once they were free of her.

"What about my underwear?" Nora asked, her voice shaky above him.

Drawing his gaze up the length of her legs, he settled on the nearly-translucent fabric shielding his view of her most private place.

Above him, Nora squirmed under his scrutiny, wafting the scent of her arousal toward him. Inhaling deeply, Endre filled his lungs with it. Gods, how he wanted to taste her, to run his tongue along the seam of her lips and collect her dew. "Do you wish me to remove them?" he asked with a smirk, prying his eyes from her mound with extreme difficulty to look her in the eyes.

"N-no," she whimpered, her expression shuttering—in an instant morphing from unadulterated desire to one of terror.

The fear in her eyes sobered him, his need dissipating into the ether. Abruptly, Endre rose to his feet, scooping the nearly-naked woman into his arms before she could topple to the ground. Silently, he stalked into the bedroom, laying his charge on the bed and stepping away quickly to erase the feel of her body pressed against him.

With his breathing erratic, he watched her struggle to pull the covers over her shaking body. He longed to help her, but feared his lust would overtake him if he came too close to her again. It took considerable effort to push visions of his face between her thighs, followed by thrusting into her warmth from his mind.

Although he had only returned to their room a short time ago, the need to depart once again clawed at him from the inside. He could not remain in the same room with her, knowing she was bare beneath the blanket and for a few moments, she had *wanted* him—without the influence of his pheromones.

Concentrating on the task at hand and only those actions, he pulled the blanket over Nora. It hid his view well enough, but it did not erase the image of her body burned into his brain or the scent of her arousal still clinging in his nostrils. "Rest," he instructed, unable to command his feet to move from the bedside. Gently, he brushed a wet tendril of hair from her forehead and took in her simple beauty. He should not touch her.

Nora stared up at him, her eyes still wide and her lips finally taking on a more healthy shade of pink. "I'm scared," she whispered.

It was impossible to decipher the source of her fear from her simple words. Was it him she feared? The disease ravaging her body? Or was it the desire for him which terrified her? As much as he wanted to hear the answer, his human was exhausted.

"Sleep," he commanded, finally able to step back from her.

Settling into a chair across the room, he watched her and waited for her breathing to deepen with sleep before slipping from the room to find another way to work out his frustrations. It seemed the Norns had doomed him to a life filled with tragedy.

CHAPTER SEVENTEEN

Nora stepped from the shower, momentarily forgetting the horrors she'd experienced over the last several days. She artfully wound a towel around her drenched hair and wrapped a second around her aching body. Between the blood loss and being manhandled, her body was really starting to show the abuse, despite the healing the Vampire blood was *supposed* to be doing. Bruises and healing lacerations formed a patchwork across her skin. She swiped her hand across the fogged mirror, knowing she would see the same exhausted face with dark circles under the eyes which were there before she entered the cascade of scalding water. Nora had hoped a shower would make her feel refreshed and give her mind a chance to absorb all that had happened since the morning in Italy—the one she'd thought was her last. But in reality, she knew the solitude of the shower would be short-lived. Endre didn't appear to like to leave her alone very long, though it seemed more as if he were concerned she'd collapse at a moment's notice than fear she'd stage a jailbreak.

The concern confused her. Well, most everything about the last several days confused her. But it was the pull to Endre which baffled her most. There were moments when she felt things other than fear. Last night, for example. They way he'd looked at her had sent heat and longing through her. There had been hunger in his gaze, a desire for more than her blood. Over the last few days, she'd thought she'd seen those same expressions on him, but they had been fleeting. But last night was the first time he'd gazed at her so openly. And she had been terrified to find she'd liked it, and wanted more than just his eyes on her.

As if on cue, the door flew open unceremoniously and her captor strode into the small bathroom unannounced. Nora didn't know why she was surprised, it seemed as though he could sense her changes in mood.

"Are you well?" he demanded, those icy eyes roving over her face, searching.

The bright blue of those orbs unnerved her, as if they could see into the very depths of her soul where her deepest, darkest desires lay hidden from the rest of the world except for him. "Yes," she whispered, casting her gaze to the floor, hoping to keep her secret intact.

"Your heartrate increased pace," he continued, ducking his head in an attempt to catch her eyes again.

She closed her eyes to block out Endre's icy stare. But that was a *very* bad idea. Every time she shut her eyes, the rapid-fire images of her nightmares assaulted her. The quickness with which they flashed through her mind was disorienting and brought on bouts of nausea.

"You look ill," Endre commented, a note of concern in his voice. "I should not have allowed you to shower on your own, your body is still very weak," he chided himself.

Her eyes snapped open when she felt him move close enough so he almost touched her, but not quite. Nora swallowed thickly to keep the rising bile down and tried to steady the teetering movement of her body. At least the room stopped spinning when her eyes were open.

Endre stood so he took up her entire field of vision. His gaze bored into hers, daring her to look anywhere else but into the blue depths. "Perhaps I should escort you to the bed."

Visions of his exquisite physique pressing her needy body into the mattress filled her mind. Just that small snippet of imagery stole her breath away and made her core clench with a need she'd never been so desperate to fulfill.

A slow smile broke across his lips, and Nora's eyes immediately flicked to the canines waiting to inflict pain. She couldn't pry her eyes from the gleaming daggers; even as he circled her, her eyes followed his mischievous smile. When he stopped behind her, she held her breath, bracing herself for the inevitable pain of his bite.

Nuzzling his nose along the sensitive skin of her neck, he skimmed right along the healing puncture wounds from his last feeding. A deep, satisfied groan sounded from him when he drew in a deep lungful of her scent, vibrating the sound through her body. "Gods, you smell good."

Something had shifted between them last night when he tended to her mysterious wound and cared for her when her body succumbed to shock. A delighted shiver ran through her when she thought back to the way his eyes drank in her naked body and the desire they held. Though she remained his captive, in those moments, it was as if she held the same sway over his body as he did over hers. It terrified her—the raw *need* in his gaze, along with her body's reciprocation and willingness to give in to it.

Endre's warm hands caressed her arms and massaged her shoulders while his lips played along the planes of her neck.

A low moan sounded from somewhere deep in her throat.

Running his hands along her arms, and up over her exposed collarbone sent a delighted shiver through her, her skin tingling from his touch. His hands continued their exploration, back down her arms, and along the luxurious fabric of the towel still wrapped up over her chest.

It was as if his movements were the secret code her body and mind required to give in to this *need* he'd awoken in her. Unthinking, only feeling, Nora released her death-grip on the towel tucked around her.

A sharp intake of breath sounded from him when the terrycloth fluttered to her feet. His movements behind her froze.

Nora's heart kicked in her chest and her breath came in quick gasps. Was she really going to do this? Give her body and innocence to this Vampire? Did he even want that? Or was it merely more of her blood he was after?

"Why, little lamb, I can hear your heart. Is it from fear or anticipation, I wonder?" he whispered in her ear.

A shiver ran through her body. Nora was tempted to close her eyes again, just to escape into the visions of her nightmares from the growing tension between them. The warring emotions between longing for his touch and fearing his rejection filled her like a balloon near to bursting. Amidst the internal battle, she was vaguely aware of his hands trailing up and down her sides with feather-light touches. She began feeling more self-conscious with every flaw on display to his sharp eyes. If he noticed them, he didn't say.

His breath came quicker now, too. Which either meant he felt the same desire for her, or the culmination of her pain was only moments away and he was going to bite her.

Endre's lips trailed along her neck and Nora found herself tilting her head ever so slightly to give him better access. He murmured unintelligibly into her neck and pulled away for what she assumed was the strike. Her whole body tensed, just waiting. But Nora never felt his bite.

He stood behind her, gripping her shoulders painfully, keeping her at arm's length away, his breathing nearly as heavy as her own. "I cannot, I have already taken too much," he whispered.

Nora's body began to shake then, whether from cold, relief, or the unspent adrenaline coursing through her body, she wasn't sure.

Endre reached to the floor and retrieved the fallen towel.

Nora noticed at some point the towel from her hair ended up on the floor as well. He brushed her hair over to one shoulder and she thought he was going to place the towel around her, but instead he went still, his fingertips still resting on her skin. Glancing up at their reflection in the now-clear mirror, she saw his gaze riveted on what she could only assume was the tattoo covering most of her back.

"What is this?" he questioned her softly.

"A tree. The Norse World Tree," Nora answered hoarsely.

"I know *what* it is, but why is Yggdrasil on your back, Nora?" he prompted, dropping the towel to the floor.

She couldn't decipher the tone in his voice. Nora watched curiously in the mirror as he stared at the black ink swirled across her skin and startled when his fingers traced the lines of the branches.

"What compelled you to adorn your skin with such an image?" he questioned, his eyes never leaving her back.

Nora cleared her throat to get her bearings in the conversation. She was having a hard time following his rapt interest in her ink. "My grandmother was full-blooded Norwegian and I like the mythology, I like the stories and the symbolism. They remind me of her, of the stories she used to tell. Those stories are one of the reasons I wanted to go into the field of archaeology, old culture fascinates me."

"There is imagery aplenty to choose from, why this? Why Yggdrasil?"

"I also love nature, especially trees since they are symbolic of life—which I am quite fond of," she explained, the last coming out with a note of bitterness in her tone.

"Trees can also bring death. A tree can be used as a crypt, for example. Or, they were often times used in hangings. There are even trees which excrete toxins from their roots to kill surrounding plants. You see, all life is tainted with death. Life is a circle, a vicious and equal cycle with death," he said, tracing the lines of the roots just above the curve of her backside.

Now she understood what caught his attention. The tree imprinted on her skin was a dark effigy of the one which had imprisoned him for decades with its twisted branches and gnarled bark.

"Do you believe in those gods whose world is built upon this tree, Nora?"

"No. They're just stories of a long dead religion."

"It was my religion," he divulged with a sigh, "But you are correct, so many of the intricacies have been diminished to mere tales over the centuries."

"Vampires don't have their own religion?" she queried, her attention as rapt on him and the conversation as his was on tracing the ink on her skin.

"I was not always a Vampire," he reminded her. "And though you claim the beliefs of my old life are dead, I still carry part of them with me. I still think about them, superstitious as many of the ideas are. But I suppose everyone needs something to believe in."

"What do you believe?" she whispered, completely unsure what to expect for an answer.

"I believe I belong here," he testified, regret edging his tone as he traced the furthest tip of the roots on the tree right above her butt cheek, "in Helheim. I am a soulless creature, doomed to live my afterlife in Hel. There will be no Valhalla for me. I do not want that for you," he whispered. "Your light should never be subjected to Hel, but what choice do I have?"

Nora's body quaked and broke out in goose bumps at his touch. The movement broke whatever trance held him captivated and he draped the discarded towel around her shoulders, which she immediately clasped it to cover herself.

When he came around to face her, the softness in his eyes was gone in an instant, replaced with such an intensity of self-loathing and hatred that she couldn't help but shrink away from him.

"I truly am one of those monsters from your grandmother's stories. Perhaps it is time to remind us both what kind of creature I am." Roughly, he latched onto her upper arm and dragged her from the bathroom.

"Wait, no, please!" Nora cried out as she stumbled behind him. "You're not a monster."

"Patronizing me will not change what I am. This is for the best," he bemoaned, his voice catching in his throat, his expression twisted in anguish.

"Please don't kill me," Nora begged, unashamed as she pled for her life.

The Vampire shook his head. "No, not tonight." In a matter of seconds, he ripped the cord from one of the lamps and bound her hands together. He lashed them to the metal posts of the bed, her hands artfully framed between the rungs.

"You don't have to do this," she protested, her mind a whirl from the sudden change in atmosphere from desire-charged to this insane mixture of anger, pain, and loathing he radiated.

"Yes, I do. I have to feed elsewhere tonight. I have taken too much from you, if I take any more, your body will continue to weaken and your wounds will cease to heal and your illness will only progress faster. I also cannot have you running off without me. You will never survive."

"I won't run, I promise," Nora lied, struggling against the biting cord.

"I cannot risk that. If I believed for a moment you would listen to reason and stay put, I would leave you here to your own devices and conduct my business. Though we have spent a short amount of time together, I know you, Nora. It is not in your nature to sit idly by when an opportunity presents itself. You may believe my absence is the key to your salvation, but outside these walls are more dangers than you can fathom. Your unfortunate association with me has now made you a target for my enemies. I cannot allow you to fall into the hands of Lorenzo or his cretins."

"I'll stay put," she protested, even as she struggled against the cord binding her wrists.

"It is out of the question."

"Ple—" The rough fibers of a washcloth shoved into her mouth cut off any further protest.

"I regret things have to be this way. At least until…" he trailed off, tilting his head to the ceiling and shaking it slightly.

Until what? She wanted to shout at him, but her words came out as only a mumble around the cloth in her mouth. Maybe she could push it out with her tongue?

Tossing the towel which had been around her body only moments before back into the bathroom, he reminded her that not only was she bound to the bed, too weak to put up much of a struggle, she was also completely naked.

It appeared that at that moment, he remembered it too. His eyes roamed over her hungrily, speaking once more of lust and passion.

When his tongue swiped across his bottom lip to wet it, Nora's heart fluttered in response. A strange mixture of thrill and fear washed through her, but though she wanted to experience the things his gaze promised, not like this—not forced, not *taken.*

With her eyes, she pled with the man she saw beneath the monster he continued to convince her he was, *not like this.*

"You have nothing to fear from me tonight," he said, throwing a blanket over her and fashioning a gag from one of her shirts to keep the washcloth lodged in her mouth. "Though I desire you, I would never take carnal pleasure from you against your will. I am not that type of monster." Striding to the window, he slid the pane open and peered into the alley below. "Please behave while I am gone," he advised, his gaze still fixed to the pitch-black streets below. "Though you may not believe it, your best chance of survival is with me." When he turned back to her, he gave a wry smile before disappearing to prey upon some new, unsuspecting victim.

Behave? Nora seethed as she twisted and pulled at the cord around her wrists. He had been right when he said she would seize an opportunity if it presented itself, and that meant that by no means was she going to lie still and wait for his return. For hours, she contorted into every position she could conceive of, and was no closer to freedom. By the looks of things, she only succeeded in rubbing her wrists raw, and shifting the blanket half off her body, exposing her nakedness to the cold air.

Tears leaked from the corners of her eyes while she attempted to ignore the burning of her wrists and accepted the truth. Sobs wracked Nora's body as her reality sank in. She was weak. This wouldn't be one of those horrifying, yet uplifting stories where the woman in captivity manages to rescue herself. She was well and truly trapped.

Hope drained from her with each tear, along with it the building desire she felt for her captor. How dare he claim concern for her welfare, and yet leave her like this? He didn't care about her—he cared about blood and revenge. Those dark thoughts circled in her mind, a constant loop she used to keep from drifting toward sleep. The nightmares awaiting the moment she closed her eyes were incentive enough to fight exhaustion and force herself to stay awake. But her body had other ideas, and it was only a matter of time before she succumbed to sleep.

CHAPTER EIGHTEEN

Endre's frustration was mounting; they had been in the city for several days now, and yet he had been unable to gather any more information on Lorenzo's location. As he stalked dark alleyways in Paris' slums, silence met his ears. It was strange, to say the least. He expected to run into at least a few other Vampires foraging in the city, but all was relatively quiet. Of course, he ran across derelicts and vagabonds of the human variety, but none dared to give him trouble. These humans could sense the threat he posed and kept their distance. Perhaps there was something to be said about living at a baser level—they *felt* the very menace of his presence.

But where were the Vampires?

All night, Endre roamed through the streets, not once encountering another Vampire. It was as if they had all vanished into thin air and with them, any hope of finding Lorenzo. The thought had crossed his mind once or twice, questioning whether Lorenzo still lived, but the first Vampire he had interrogated did not deny knowing his whereabouts, merely refused to provide them.

The serpent was still here, Endre was sure of it. It was a matter of how to flush him out into the open to claim his revenge. By now, Lorenzo had to know Endre was here, the question was, what was he waiting for? It was unlike Lorenzo to allow anyone to stalk his city and leave behind a body count, and not seek retribution. The lightening sky to the east reminded he would not find those answers tonight. Even though the Vampires could operate in the daylight, that did not mean they *wanted* to. He had no desire to walk the streets in daylight today, and yet, he was hesitant to return to the hotel room and the quandary he was unable to push from his mind—but his frustrations must be faced.

Silently, he traversed the shadows and entered the room the same way he had left—through the window. In the quiet of the room, the only sound he could hear was the steady breathing of Nora as she slept. Sliding to the chair beside the bed, Endre propped his elbows on his knees and dropped his head into his hands. The steady rhythm of Nora's breaths should have calmed him, but instead they tormented him.

When he lifted his gaze from the floor to the sleeping woman, his chest grew tight when he looked upon her. Her wrists were twisted at an odd angle to accommodate her body's position on her side. With knees drawn up into her naked body, she shivered in the cool air. The perfume of her blood hung in the air, no doubt from the lacerations she had given herself on her wrists when she attempted escape. There was another scent too, salt. Tears. This woman was a far cry from the naked vixen he had been picturing in his mind all night as he hunted the streets.

Carefully so he did not wake her, he removed the gag from her mouth and unwound the cord from her wrists, tossing everything to the side in disgust with one hand while his other examined the wounds on her wrists. Nothing detrimental, only superficial. A few drops of his blood would heal them right up. But that brought him back to his quandary—feeding her more Vampire blood. By continuing to pour his blood down her gullet, he only delayed the inevitable. Soon, he would have to tell her what fate awaited her. The longer he delayed, the worse the fallout would be, of that he was certain.

Placing her hands to rest on the pillow beside her head, he covered her with the blanket before he took his seat again. Forcing himself not to look away, he took in Nora's tranquil face, expressionless in sleep. Her beauty was unparalleled, he would go so far as to claim her fairness surpassed that of his deceased wife

Ingrid, whose likeness to his captive was uncanny. Things had grown beyond a simple fascination with her likeness to his dead wife and blossomed into something else having nothing to do with Ingrid. Whereas he had loved his wife, his connection with Nora was something more. He was drawn to her like a moth to a flame, ever more in danger of incinerating with each glance. She had pulled him from the darkness, and now that he had been bathed in her light, he could not live without it. Therein was the crux of the issue.

The arguments he had played in his head time and again began their loop, but this time he contemplated a possibility not yet dwelt upon. He had already come to terms with the reality Nora would transition to a Vampire, regardless of the path which brought her there. That new life would leave her devoid of the light he had come to crave. She would cease to be the woman she was now. What he had not considered until this moment was perhaps a tragic end to them both was the most appropriate answer to save her from this life of darkness—to save them both.

Selfishness warred with selflessness in him.

What was he to do?

Leaning back, he closed his eyes, allowing sleep to wash over him, sweeping away his worries for a few hours.

A whimper sounded from Nora, breaking into Endre's dreams of long-forgotten wars. The twitch of her limbs and the slight fluttering of her eyelashes brought him to the edge of his chair.

A blood memory.

Endre had watched over her while her dream jolted her body and elicited agonizing sounds from her throat. The noises hinted at the excruciating pain she felt in the recesses of her mind, wounds she now felt as vividly as he had when they were originally inflicted upon him. Though, thankfully, she had not had any of those wounds follow her into the waking world since the last incident. Still, he could not stop the memories from bombarding her. The pain of his past was now being exacted upon her. All of the dark, bloody horrors of his history were yet to play through her mind. Soon, he would not be able to hold on to his secrets—she would know and experience them all.

Remorse stirred in his chest. Without the administration of his blood, she would never have been subjected to this hell.

A guttural scream drew his attention back to the woman on the bed. Hotel security would be sent up if she continued. The thought of gagging her again crossed his mind, but he decided attempting to wake her was a better idea. Endre tenderly brushed the backs of his fingers along Nora's cheek. He would allow himself this moment of weakness while she was not awake to witness it. There was no hope of avoiding the connection he felt to her, only deciding what to do about it.

CHAPTER NINETEEN

Nora jolted awake from her fevered dream, panting and drenched in sweat, the thin blanket clinging to her naked body.

"What did you see?" a quiet voice demanded of her in the dark. It was always the same question.

She had been in a box. The dream had started in dull blackness, and at first, her emotions were heightened without her sight. Nora felt tidal wave after alternating tidal wave of fear, anger, and loneliness. She could feel the pressure of the earth all around her. She could hear the sounds of the outside world above her, just beyond her reach. An unlucky rodent had found its way into her prison, and Nora gagged remembering draining its blood in her dream. She had also eaten insects as they gnawed away at the wood and intruded in on her. When she looked at the clock, she had only been asleep for a few hours, but time seemed to pass differently in the dream, and she felt like she was there for *years.*

"I don't know what's real anymore. Am I going crazy? My dreams feel so real," Nora whispered into the suffocating blackness, reminiscent of the prison from her dream.

"If you are mad, then so am I. *Folie à deux*, a shared madness." Endre chuckled from the shadows. "They are not dreams."

"They're memories, aren't they?" Nora replied in the direction she sensed his voice came from.

She didn't know how—after all that time he spent in the darkness of his tomb—he could stand to sit here, enveloped by it without panicking.

"My memories, my wounds, yes." His voice came softly.

"That—you had to live through that? I–I felt like I was there, it was so dark," she choked out. "How—why are your memories in my head?" she questioned, unable to keep the quiver from her voice, or quell her rising hysteria.

"It is the blood. *My* blood," he confessed grimly.

She felt the bed shift as he moved away from her in the dark.

At least he'd untied her, she noted, trying to focus her mind elsewhere—attempting to focus anywhere but on the cloying fear of being buried alive.

She swallowed and almost got sick when the remnants of his blood, which he presumably fed to her while she was reliving his imprisonment, coated her throat. Closing her eyes, she took deep breaths in an attempt to keep from vomiting, but more images, more memories passed behind her eyelids like a rapid-fire slideshow. Darkness. Dirt. Insects. Decomposition. Overwhelming feelings of rage, thirst, and revenge battled with the imagery for her attention. All in an endless loop.

The click of the bedside lamp sounded and light illuminated in front of her eyelids, drawing her back, coaxing her from the edge of the precipice she teetered on only moments before.

"Drink this," Endre commanded.

A cold glass was pressed to Nora's lips and her eyes jerked open. First, she studied the glass to confirm its contents were merely water, and then greedily chugged it down in one breath. The cool of the liquid rushing down her parched throat was heavenly. Cautiously, she handed the glass back to him and met his icy blue gaze. "What's going to happen to me?" she demanded. Nora could fathom no scenario in which having someone else's memories crammed into her brain next to her own didn't result in losing her mind altogether.

The look he gave her resembled pity. She didn't want his pity.

He stood up from the bed and pulled a dark coat he hadn't had before from the back of one of the chairs near the little table in their room.

A shudder ran through her when Nora imagined where it had come from, one of his victims no doubt. "Are—are you leaving again?" she stammered, her fear of being left to his memories overshadowing her fear of the creature himself.

The Vampire glanced at her with confusion before striding to the window and peeking through the blinds.

The sky outside was dark, but Nora had no idea what day it was anymore. These nightmares, his memories, were making her lose track of time. Perhaps this was where the instability she saw in him came from—either that or it was the near-century underground which had unraveled him. She'd spent only hours living through his personal hell as she felt disoriented and unhinged, she could only imagine what *decades* of that torture could do to a mind. Or maybe she didn't have to imagine it and was witnessing it first-hand.

"Nowhere until I restrain you to keep you from harm's way. Why? Do you miss me when I am gone, pet?" He crooked an eyebrow at her, as if he actually expected her to answer. "I am going to feed. I have been waiting for you to wake since dawn. It is now dusk and I am hungry and have information to hunt down," he grumbled.

At the mention of his hunger, her stomach rumbled.

With a frown, he turned back to her. "When was the last time you ate?" he demanded.

The question perplexed Nora. She hadn't eaten in *days*. All she'd had to consume since they'd arrived in this godforsaken room was his blood. "Like, food?" she questioned slowly, wondering if this was a trick question. She didn't do anything without him watching over her like a hawk. Surely, he would know he hadn't fed her in several days.

"Yes, food, Nora." A frown creased his brows as he searched her face.

"Since before we got here," she whispered, holding back tears. It was the exhaustration getting to her again. Days without food and only blood to survive on, not to mention she hadn't had a decent night's sleep since before this whole thing began, was taking its toll.

Sighing, he picked up a menu from the small table in the corner and dropped it into her lap. "Forgive me, I have forgotten your human need to eat," he apologized with another sigh. "Order whatever you desire."

Glancing at the menu, Nora bit her lip in embarrassment. It was written in French. She couldn't read French. "Um..." she hesitated, staring at the laminated piece of paper. "I can't read this."

Taking the menu from her, he scanned the writing before placing it on the table. "What would you like to eat?" he questioned.

"I don't know, what's on there?" Nora inquired, not sure how she was supposed to answer.

Endre peered up at her from under his brows, clearly annoyed, and stepped toward her. It seemed he was a bit on the side of hangry.

"A burger. Or steak. I've been craving red meat," Nora answered quickly to halt his advance.

Nodding, his face took on a thoughtful expression. "Your blood is deficient in iron."

"I suppose you would know," she mumbled, glancing away.

With a sigh, he picked up the phone on the bedside table and spoke in French, presumably to place the food order. "Your food will arrive shortly," he informed her when he replaced phone handset in the cradle.

"Do you ever eat food?" she asked curiously.

Endre resumed his post in the chair beside the bed, fixing her with an annoyed glare. "No."

"Do you miss it?"

For a moment, it looked as though he wasn't going to answer. Pursing his lips, he considered her question for a moment, then answered, "It has been over a thousand years since I have ingested anything other than blood. My memories of how food tastes are vague, at best. It is difficult to miss something I hardly recall."

Nora nodded. "What do you do when you're not hunting out there?" she blurted out, turning her gaze from where her fingers twisted in her lap against the blanket to where he watched her.

"I am looking for someone."

"Lorenzo?" Nora recalled from an earlier conversation.

"Yes." Endre nodded solemnly. "The only way to ensure he is not a threat to either of us is to find him first."

"What happens when you find him?" she asked, her voice tremulous because she suspected she already knew the answer.

A knock sounded at the door before Endre could answer, and suddenly she was fearful for whoever was on the other side.

Endre took three long strides and was at the door. He opened it with a smile designed to hide his fangs and spoke pleasantly with the attendant, taking the tray from her, but barring her from stepping farther into the room than the doorway.

When the door closed and he turned toward her with the tray, Nora let out a relieved breath.

Endre gave her a smile and a chuckle. "It would be most unwise to feed from the hotel staff, do you not you think?" Setting the tray on her lap, he pulled the cover off the plate with a flourish.

The smell of cooked meat hit Nora's nostrils, making her mouth water—she was ravenous. Picking up the burger, she took enormous bites, almost too big to chew, swallowing large chunks whole.

"You are going to choke," Endre offered from where he sat, watching her eat.

Slowing, Nora took another bite and savored it. As she chewed, she let the food roll around her mouth to catalogue each flavor. It tasted strange. Swallowing a mouthful, she peeled back the bun to look at the burger. It was cooked just how she liked it, but there was something off about the taste.

"Is there a problem with your food?" he demanded from his perch on one of the chairs.

"It tastes…strange. Maybe it's grass-fed or the meat's bad. I don't know, I can't pinpoint what it is," she contemplated, wrinkling her nose as she stared down at her burger.

"The meat is not bad, Nora. I would have smelled that," he refuted with a scowl. "You need to eat to regain strength."

"What is it?" she watched him closely, noting the way he would not meet her eyes. "There's something you're not telling me."

"Eat," he commanded and rose from the chair again, his expression remaining distraught.

Nora took another bite and chewed slowly as she watched him.

He leaned against the window and motioned her to hurry.

"Is the information you're gathering for this revenge plan you've told me nothing about?" Nora prompted curiously before taking another bite of her burger and ignoring the odd taste.

"Yes," he replied stiffly.

"So, what *is* this plan, then?" Nora probed after swallowing. He had been stalking through the night since they got to Paris, in pursuit of information for this elusive plan he'd kept secret. She intended to get some information out of him, especially if he expected her to participate in some way. There was no way she was going on some revenge-suicide mission without knowing what she was in for. Not that he'd given her much of a choice anyway.

"The plan is to find Lorenzo and kill him," Endre declared with a nonchalant shrug.

"Sounds simple enough. But you haven't found him," Nora pointed out, taking another bite.

"If I had found him, he would be dead, and so would you," he snapped at her. "Hurry up, woman. I would like dinner as well," he said, exasperated.

The lump of meat sat heavy in her stomach, her guts roiling with his words, her appetite lost. Just when it seemed they made some progress, he reminded her of her impending demise.

"Go relieve yourself," he commanded, gesturing to the bathroom.

Stiffly, Nora rose to her feet.

"Quickly. Leave the door open," he ordered, his gaze wary.

It took considerable effort to keep the food in her stomach where it belonged, but she managed to do so as she rushed through her bathroom routine. When she stepped back into the room, he waited for her with cord in hand, ready to bind her to the headboard again. She took a step back toward the bathroom.

"I cannot have you running away while I am gone," he insisted, catching her wrist with one hand and dragging her toward the bed.

"No! Please, I'll stay right here. Where would I go? I don't know anything about Paris," Nora pleaded as she dug her heels into the thin carpet and pried at his fingers with her nails

"The abrasion on your wrists from your escape attempts last night tell a different story," he countered, yanking her toward him.

Nora stumbled into him, her hands landing on his expansive chest.

Locking his arms around her, he pulled her into a crushing embrace. "I cannot risk your safety," he whispered, his voice and gaze softening as he peered down at her. Unwinding an arm from her, he pushed a lock of hair from her eyes.

Glancing up into the earnest expression on his face, she swallowed thickly at the intimate position, her body betraying her desire for his with the heat growing between her legs. "If what you say is true, I'll never be safe as long as I'm with you."

"No," he acknowledged, shaking his head. "If you are out there, I cannot protect you. At least here, I know where you are."

"How do you know they won't come here for me as soon as you leave?"

A furrow formed between his brows, as if he hadn't considered the possibility his enemies might already know where he was. "I would know if I had been followed. You are safest here."

"Wouldn't I be safer the farther I am away from you?" she pushed, her gaze dropping to his full bottom lip.

"Unlikely," he said, bending her body so she lay on the bed, his weight atop her.

"Please let me go," she pleaded in a whisper, her eyes searching his for some shred of decency, some compassion to appeal to.

"I cannot do that. You could be a thousand kilometers from me, and your life would still be in danger. Your fate is sealed," he murmured, planting a kiss on her neck and pressing his hips into hers.

"What does that mean?" she asked breathlessly, letting out a moan as he ran his hands down the sides of her body, brushing his fingers along her breasts. It was clear he was trying to distract her, and doing a damn good job at it, too. "You don't have to kill me," she choked on the words as they left her throat, her desire dissipating into the ether.

"Even if I do not, your body will turn against you." The Vampire leaned back to meet her gaze.

Nora didn't like what she saw there—pity. "Because of your blood?" she demanded, pushing against his chest in an attempt to dislodge him. Her efforts accomplished nothing.

Without a word, Endre caught her wrists and pulled her arms above her head.

"Tell me what you did to me!" Nora howled, twisting her wrists in his grip and bucking her hips attempting to dislodge him.

"Nora, stop. I do not wish to hurt you," he said, pressing her body harder into the mattress with his own.

"What did you do to me?" she screamed, kicking and thrashing beneath him.

"I am trying to protect you," he insisted, lifting his body slightly while he dragged her up the bed toward the headboard.

"Fuck you!" she screeched, kicking at him, her knee catching him in the groin.

Letting out a pained groan, his grip on her loosened a fraction.

Taking advantage of the situation, Nora reared back to strike at him again. Before she could strike, all the breath was pushed from her lungs when his body flattened atop her once more. "Get off of me," she growled at him through clenched teeth. "Don't you fucking touch me!"

Fire replaced the ice in his gaze and with deft movements, he bound her to the bed as he had the night before.

It all happened faster than Nora could follow.

"Try to rest," he told her, pushing off the bed and striding to the window.

"Go back to your Hel!" she spat.

Her words stilled him a few feet from the window. Slowly, he turned back toward her, his eyes narrowed and his lip curled up enough she could see a single fang glistening in the light.

Nora shrank back into cushion of the pillow at the malevolence in his expression. As pissed as she was at him right now for well, everything, she wouldn't curse her worst enemy with being buried alive for almost a century. A few hours in his memory of it had been too much for her.

With slow stalking strides, he approached the bed.

She'd been afraid of him before, but in recent days, she'd seen a different side of him, something more—human. This, the creature before her was once again the monster she dug up from his grave. It was as if the very mention of burying him back in that hole undid the progression from a crazed lunatic to the semi-stable Vampire she'd seen over the last few days.

"You have been there and yet, you would send me back?" Pain softened his expression from rage. He looked *betrayed*.

"I—" Nora was unable to finish her retraction before he shoved cloth of some kind into her mouth.

"Since you cannot control your mouth," he said with a sigh, and sat on the edge of the bed beside her.

Nora watched him warily, sure he was going to snap at any moment, her fear clawing at her throat the closer he got to her.

"I understand it is hard to see the reasons behind my actions. They may seem cruel, but I will continue to reassure you, they are for your well-being." Bending toward her, he pressed a kiss to her forehead.

Without her permission, her eyelids fluttered shut. The sensation of his lips burning a trail up her neck and along her jaw sent tingles racing across her skin, leaving her lightheaded.

"I will return soon," he whispered, placing another kiss on her forehead as he ran the backs of his knuckles over her cheek.

CHAPTER TWENTY

When Nora opened her eyes, Endre was nowhere in sight. Tingles still radiated from where his lips brushed along her skin. Drawing in a shaking breath, she attempted to chase them away. His touch felt too good and his words sort of made sense. They shouldn't make sense. Experiencing his memories allowed her to relate to him, to see where he was coming from.

She didn't *want* to see things from his perspective. He took her captive and drank her blood. Logically, she should want to be as far away from him as possible—and yet, the idea of leaving left a pit in her stomach. For that very reason, she had to get away from him.

Despite the growing numbness in her hands, Nora fought against the cord. Taking a deep breath to quell her panic, she attempted to analyze her bonds much like she would do with any other puzzle. Endre had given her more slack in the cord tonight, not a lot, but it was enough to allow her escape. Lining up her wrists so her palms pressed together, she was able to slip one hand from her bonds—but not without a sacrifice of blood and skin. With a muffled cry of triumph, she slipped a raw and bloody wrist through the loop. The other wrist slid to the bed, her arms too heavy and numb from the lack of circulation to hold their own weight.

A quick glance at the clock as she scrambled from the bed told her Endre had been gone less than a half hour. He was usually gone for a few hours at a time, but Nora wasn't naïve enough to believe there wasn't a chance he could show up at any moment.

It took less than three minutes for her to pull on clothes. It took significantly more time for her to formulate an escape plan. Now that she was free from her bonds, she had no idea where to run to. Shaking her head, she realized it didn't matter—as long as it was away from here.

Snatching her purse from where it lay beside the bed, she raced to the door, unlocking it with shaking hands. A quick peek into the hallway revealed it was empty. Even then, she self-consciously smoothed her hands over her wrists, wishing she'd taken a few seconds to wipe the blood from them.

Doubt coaxed her back to the room for a fraction of a second—was she doing the right thing by leaving? Endre insisted she wasn't safe without him, but her logical mind reminded her it could all be a ruse. An elaborate lie concocted in an attempt to do exactly what she was about to—escape.

A deep inhale fortified her decision and she sprinted toward the stairs. The longer she dawdled, the greater the chance he would return and thwart her flight. Pushing through the fire door, she pounded down the steps until she reached the ground floor. The door she pushed through brought her into a hallway identical to the one floors above. Without a falter in her stride, she rushed toward the exterior door leading to her freedom. There was no need to go to the lobby and involve the authorities, that would only get more people killed.

The air was cool and damp when Nora emerged onto the street, the rain having slowed to a drizzle. With brisk strides, she rounded the corner into a dimly lit back street. Up ahead, bright street lights could be seen, and she headed toward them, her anxiety urging her away from the dark alleys where Endre or other Vampires like him might be lurking. Lights usually meant people, and the possibility of catching a cab to the nearest bus station or airport to get her the fuck out of Paris.

As Nora rounded a corner onto another side street, a faint growl sounded from behind a dumpster.

Nope.

Turning back the way she had come, she hoped it was only some stray dog protecting its meal.

Luck never seemed to be on her side.

A steel-like arm wrapped around her midsection, and a hand clamped over her mouth before she could let out a scream. Struggling with every ounce of strength she possessed was futile as the assailant dragged her toward the dumpster.

"Mmmm *sucré*," a voice rasped in her ear.

Nora let out a muffled cry as fangs sank into her still-tender throat.

The creature pulled back suddenly, an expression of curiosity masking his features, but distracting him enough to loosen his grip on her.

Taking advantage of the opportunity, Nora drove her elbow toward his ribs.

But he was too quick. Pinning her arms to her sides, he dragged her farther into the alley and away from the streetlights. He whispered ominously into her ear.

She didn't understand the words, but the foreboding in his tone told her everything she needed to know—his intentions were sinister. Panic crept up her spine, her skin breaking out into a cold sweat. Redoubling her efforts with what little strength she possessed, she twisted and thrashed in his grip.

A snarl ripped through him, and the band of his arm tightened across her chest, squeezing the air from her lungs.

Black spots appeared at the edges of her vision.

"I would sincerely like to know how you came to be in this alley, Nora," a familiar voice spoke from behind her.

Relief flooded through her, nearly bringing her to tears.

"Ah, so this is *your* pet," the creature still holding her mused with a chuckle when he turned them to face Endre.

"Release her without further harm and I will allow you to live," Endre responded in a menacing tone.

The Vampire holding her shook with laughter. "And if I don't? If I snap her neck now? You wouldn't reach her before her lifeless body hit the ground."

A low rumbling growl filled the expanse of the alley. "You would not live to take another breath."

"Lorenzo would be interested to know how protective you have become of the human." A taunt echoed in the Vampire's tone.

"If Lorenzo so much as touches her…" Endre's voice was more than threatening.

Another laugh rippled through her assailant's body. "You would have to find him first, before you could carry out your empty threat."

Sharp, stabbing pain shot through Nora's neck. Shock kept her silent for a moment before she realized it was her attacker's fangs slicing through her flesh, then a scream ripped from her throat when her brain finally processed the pain.

Just as suddenly as the agony began, it was gone and she found herself sprawled on the wet stone of the alley. As she gasped for air, the horrific sounds of flesh pounding flesh surrounded her while the two Vampires battled nearby. Quickly, she scrambled to her feet and ran for the well-lit street beyond the corridor, not daring to look behind her.

Mere feet from the street, a steely arm caught her around her middle. A startled screech left her throat, only to be cut off by a hand clamped over her mouth.

"Quiet, *Elskling*," Endre cautioned. "There may be others out here."

Nora twisted in his grip, attempting to break his hold, all the while knowing it was pointless. If he dragged her back to that hotel room, she had no doubt she was in for it. It seemed unlikely he'd allow her escape attempt to pass unpunished.

Pulling her deeper into the shadows, he whispered in her ear, "Do you see, now, that what I have been telling you is true? I wish to protect you."

Her response was to scream against his hand. She wouldn't be in this mess if it weren't for him. Darkness began to close into her vision again the more she struggled, her efforts weaker with each second.

"Godsdammit," Endre cursed through clenched teeth, tightening his hold around her. "You are going to hurt yourself."

Footsteps sounded beyond her vision, and Nora screamed louder against the Vampire's hand, hoping to catch a passerby's attention.

"We have to leave, there are more of Lorenzo's minions approaching," he cautioned. "I cannot protect you and fight them off at the same time."

All rational thought left her brain as his hand moved to cover both her nose and mouth—blocking off all air.

"I am sorry," he whispered low into her ear. "This is the only way I can get us both out of here safely if you will not cease struggling."

The noises around her grew muffled. The little light seeping into the shadows of the alley shrunk away as a different kind of darkness took over her vision.

"Forgive me," came Endre's voice from somewhere under the depths of darkness.

CHAPTER TWENTY-ONE

Nora's body went limp in Endre's arms, and for a brief moment of panic, his heart ceased to beat while he listened for the draw of her lungs and the pumping of her blood. Relief passed through him when the familiar pulsing resumed.

The sounds of footsteps thundered down the alley, shattering his relief. He had known it was only a matter of time before he had found Lorenzo—or Lorenzo had found him—but it had never been in the plans for Nora to be present.

Tossing Nora over his shoulder, he artfully scaled a gate into a fenced-off alley and ran. Weaving, he attempted to avoid splashing through puddles, but it was nearly impossible. Shouts sounded from behind, but he kept his focus on the pathway ahead. It would only slow him down if he turned to look. He did not need to. Their thundering footsteps had him counting two Vampires. If it had not been for Nora and the loss of her blood to the now-dead Vampire lying in the alley, Endre would have been able to take care of his two pursuers. He could not risk setting her down to deal with them, only to have a third snatch her away while he was distracted. It was exactly the kind of trick Lorenzo would employ.

The sounds of pursing Vampires died away as Endre sped through the alleyways, his centuries of survival allowing him to outpace them, even while carrying Nora. Careful not to lead them directly to the hotel, he circumnavigated the building, though he did not doubt Lorenzo knew the location they were staying by now. A growl erupted from him when he considered this encounter might have been his lone chance to interrogate his enemy's men. Tonight was the closest he had come to locating Lorenzo.

At last, when he could no longer hear or smell the other Vampires, he circled back toward the hotel. A moment of hesitation stalled him a block from the building. The wisest course of action, to keep Lorenzo from using Nora as bait would be to find a new location from which to continue his investigations. Endre did not doubt Lorenzo would find them again, but as long as his enemy knew where they were staying, he could not leave his human charge alone. Even if she were not prone to escape attempts, Endre would not put it past Lorenzo to use Nora as leverage to flush him out.

A plan began to formulate in his mind, perhaps this situation could be turned to his advantage. Rather than allow Lorenzo the upper hand by using Nora as a means to capture or kill Endre, he could turn the tables and do the same—use Nora as bait to draw Lorenzo out. It was unlikely she would agree to such a plan, perhaps the best course of action would be to simply omit the details.

Leaping from the ground, Endre landed lightly on the windowsill outside their room. It would take very little time to pack their bags and move to a new location. Laying Nora on the bed, he began hastily stuffing clothing and items scattered from the floor into the bags. The ruse would be more believable if Lorenzo thought they were merely moving to another hotel.

A groan from Nora brought Endre's attention away from the bags and his thoughts.

Her brow was pinched in pain, the lacerations on her neck still open and bleeding.

Swallowing thickly, he glanced away in an attempt to quell the saliva pooling in his mouth at the mere sight of the crimson liquid. It took several deep breaths before he could look in her direction again. The wound was not healing, despite the large volume of his blood which should still be lurking in her system. Curse that sickness of hers, draining her of life. His plan to lure Lorenzo from the shadows depended on her being able to at least keep herself standing. If he took her out into the streets now, the only thing he would accomplish would be to sentence her to a quick death at the hands of a Vampire with significantly less control over their thirst than him.

Rising from where he crouched above their luggage, Endre strode to the bed. The sight of her features twisted in such pain made his chest tighten. Slicing across his wrist with a fang, he held it to her mouth in the hopes it would ease her agony, if only temporarily. Brushing her hair back from her face, he smoothed a fingertip over the furrow between her brows, the pull in his chest loosening as her face relaxed with each small swallow.

"That is it, lamb, drink," he crooned while he petted her hair.

In reality, the best chance of survival for the both of them would be to begin her transformation to Vampire *before* facing Lorenzo. However, though he would not have to protect her as a frail human from Lorenzo's minions, the transition could be quite disorientating. He may not have to guard a human, but a newly transformed Vampire may not be much better.

"Rest, we will leave soon," Endre whispered, wiping the blood from the corners of her mouth with his thumb. He was not ready to see blood as a constant fixture on her lips. A few hours' rest would not make the likelihood of finding Lorenzo any less.

CHAPTER TWENTY-TWO

"**Elskling,** *it is time* to go," a voice whispered in Nora's ear from somewhere nearby.

Elskling? Confusion settled around her, a million questions pinging around in her brain. "Go?" she questioned as she attempted to open her eyes. It was hard, her eyelids must be made of lead to be so heavy.

"Yes, we need to relocate somewhere Lorenzo's men will not find us so easily."

"Another hotel?" A yawn escaped with her murmured words.

"Lamb, open your eyes," Endre coaxed.

"I can't," she protested, giving a valiant attempt.

"You can." His voice held an unmistakable edge to it.

"Just a few more minutes."

"Nora, we must leave if you wish to survive Paris and Lorenzo's men," Endre warned while he pressed a finger against her throat. "He knows we are here, he will send his minions here."

"Ow," she hissed when Endre brushed a finger over the bite marks from her attacker in the alleyway.

"If you had stayed where I left you, you would not be in such pain," he chided, removing his touch. "When will you realize I am protecting you?"

An indelicate snort of disbelief escaped Nora before she could check it. Gagging and tying her up were in the name of protection now. "I still don't understand why," she murmured. "What difference does it make if Lorenzo or his men kill me, or if you do?"

"You still have not figured it out," he said with a sigh.

"Figured *what* out?" Cautiously, she pried her eyelid open a crack to see him, hoping a glimpse of his expression might give her a better clue as to what the fuck was going on when his words didn't.

"I am rather fond of you."

Another snort of derision. "Don't you mean you're rather fond of my blood? If you were fond of me, you wouldn't drag me along on your crusade against a centuries old enemy and let me go."

"We are long past that point, lamb. If I were to release you, what do you think would be the first thing Lorenzo would do?" he questioned, moving so his blue eye peered into her half open green one.

"He'd kill me." The answer seemed simple enough.

"No." Endre shook his head slowly, his expression dour. "He would capture you. Then he would torture you with the hopes of drawing my location from you. Or, he would simply wait."

"For?"

"Me to come for you."

A mirthless laugh rippled through her. "He'd be better off killing me, I suppose." Dread pooled in her gut. Every conversation these days had such a grim edge to it, always resulting in a conclusion involving death. When had her life become so dark?

"Did I not come for you in the alley?"

He had, but the fuzzy cloud covering her brain wasn't letting her see the point of all this.

"Lorenzo sees what you do not. My rescue of you in that alley gave him the perfect leverage. *You.* If you were merely a food source, there would be no need for me to risk life and limb fighting his guards to retrieve you," he said, speaking in more riddles she couldn't figure out.

"I don't understand the point you're trying to make." The pieces floated closer together, but the picture wasn't any clearer. Nora squeezed her eyes closed and gave her head a little shake. The answer was right there, just beyond her reach, but she couldn't see it.

"Nora, I care for you. *Deeply*."

Nora's stomach swooped and her breath hitched. She was at the top of a rollercoaster, watching all the cars in front of her drop off into the abyss, knowing it was mere seconds before her turn arrived to experience the weightlessness of falling.

"Nora," he whispered, cradling her cheek in his palm.

Light strokes over her cheek marked where he caressed her. This couldn't be real. Was he saying what she thought he was saying?

"Nora," he called to her again. "Open your eyes. Look at me."

She didn't want to open her eyes, one glimpse of any sincerity in his expression would make his declaration real.

"Please, Nora," he pleaded, his voice cracking. "Look me in the eye and tell me you feel nothing for me. Tell me you harbor not a single fond emotion for me."

For the first time since he woke her, both Nora's eyes were open. Wide. Staring at him.

How *did* she feel about him?

Her eyes roamed over his face, his impossibly handsome features. No one should be allowed to be this good-looking. It simply wasn't fair. The sight of his pleading blue eyes set her heart thumping hard in her chest. "I don't know what you want me to say," Nora whispered, her gaze dropping to his lips. At least they were easier to look at, tempting as they were, than the expectation in those blue pools.

How had things come to this?

Just days ago, he attacked her and took her prisoner with the intention of keeping her alive merely to drink her blood. Things had shifted in a seismic way. Now he saved her from attacks and claimed 'feelings?' This was hardly the same Vampire who she'd unearthed in Italy.

"Nothing?" He pulled her into a sitting position, lifting her chin gently so her eyes met his.

"No." She attempted to shake her head, but he held her firm gently, keeping her from avoiding his intense stare. It wasn't that she felt *nothing*, but she didn't have the same feelings for him that he possessed for her.

"Then, what?"

"I-I don't know how to articulate it," she stammered, pushing through the cobwebs in her mind in search of the words. They were there, she knew they were, she just had to find them and piece them together. Formulating her own thoughts into speech was almost as difficult as deciphering his riddles earlier.

"Do you hate me? For what I have done?"

"No!" she replied quickly, probably too quickly. The last thing she wanted to do was provoke him while he lurked in this emotionally vulnerable space.

"Truth, *Elskling*."

She stared at him wide-eyed and even wider-mouthed. This entire conversation caught her off guard and the only thing she could think of was to lie to him in hopes that it appeased him and he didn't see through her. His eyes bored into her as he waited, patiently. There was no way she would get a lie past those eyes. He'd lived for over a thousand years, it would be impossible to pull the wool over his eyes. "I don't love you, if that's what you're asking," she answered in an almost inaudible whisper, daring to meet his eyes again.

"I do not know how you ever could." His gaze dropped to her lips. "I have done terrible things. I have taken your life from you."

"Not yet, you haven't. I'm still alive, aren't I?"

He glanced up at her from beneath his brows.

Nora sucked in a startled breath at the intense sorrow there. Oh God, was this the part where he killed her? Made good on his promise to drain her body of blood and leave her an empty husk? "Is that how you want to protect me from Lorenzo? By killing me?" A sob rattled her words, and she covered her mouth with her hand to stifle more. Closing her eyes, she turned her face away, hot tears leaving a trail down her cheeks. "How will you do it? Will it hurt?" Was it better to know how she was going to die? Maybe it was best to not see it coming.

"You hate me."

The agony in his voice clenched like a vice around her heart, squeezing the breath from her. "I don't hate you," Nora choked out around a sob, shaking her head and sending more rivulets coursing across her cheeks. She was surprised the words spilling from her lips were the truth.

"How could you not?" he pressed, a vulnerable edge to his voice.

He was right, she had every reason to hate him. For the things he'd done to her. To her classmates and professor. To every person he'd threatened along the way, whether they knew they were in danger or not. And yet, for whatever reason, hate was not the first emotion she associated with him. Somehow, the memories of his she'd seen in her dreams gave her insight into the incredibly complicated creature in front of her. Those memories helped her to understand why he'd done some of the things he had. They'd given her a glimpse of the man beneath the monster.

"Do you *want* me to hate you?" Nora pressed, furrowing her brow as she attempted to decipher yet another riddle. "Will it make it easier to take my life?"

"No," he scoffed. "Of course not."

"Then what are you waiting for?" Anger simmered in her veins when she turned to face him. "Get it over with already."

"I am not going to kill you," he told her, brushing his knuckles lightly over her cheek, gathering her tears and wiping them away.

Nora scowled at him while she watched his expression, waiting for the monster to reappear where a torn man knelt beside her. "You've said you would, almost from the moment I found you."

"I cannot," he said with a slight shake of his head, his eyes locked on her lips. "I will do everything in my power to save you."

Breath caught in Nora's throat as Endre leaned nearer, his lips nearly touching hers. Her heart beat within its cage as his breath whispered over her lips, stealing the air from her lungs. "Kiss me," she demanded in a whisper, surprised, but not ashamed of her boldness. With eyelids fluttering closed, anticipation sent blood hammering through her heart.

A sigh left her the moment his lips touched hers. With gentle caresses, his mouth explored hers, chasing away any thoughts she had outside of how good it felt.

Gentle morphed to needy, his teeth nipping at her lower lip. "Nora," he groaned, rolling her to her back so he hovered above her, his body pressing her into the mattress.

The weight of his form against hers and the need in his voice sent blood rushing to the valley between her thighs.

His lips skimmed down the column of her throat. Warm fingers carefully tugged the collar of her shirt down over her shoulder, his mouth leaving a blazing trail in their wake.

"Ooooh," she moaned as he continued his journey to the top of her breasts and he pressed his pelvis into hers, his hard length evident beneath his jeans.

Warm hands ventured beneath the fabric of her shirt, sending a delighted shudder through her when he cupped her breast, giving it a gentle squeeze. His thumb brushed over her hardening nipple and she couldn't figure out where to focus—on his mouth licking, sucking, and kissing along her collarbone, or his hands exploring beneath her shirt.

A moment later, his mouth was gone, drawing her from her pleasurable daze. When she pried her eyes open, she caught sight of the most mischievous smile she'd ever seen on his face. With yank, he tore her shirt down the middle, rending a gasp from her.

"Holy shit, that was hot," she breathed out, her eyes wide as she stared at him.

With a grin, he lowered his mouth back to her skin, and her toes curled as he continued charting her body with his lips. Nora laced her hand in his hair, tugging involuntarily when his mouth closed over her nipple.

A pleased moan rumbled through him, sending vibrations through her, straight down to her clit.

"*Elskling*, you taste so good," he murmured against her chest. "I cannot wait to taste the rest of you."

Nora's heart jumped for a moment, temporarily clearing the haze. Was he going to drink from her again? Her muscles stiffened in anticipation of the pain until she realized his path was continuing southward. Ohhhh, he was going to do *that*. She'd never even let John put his mouth down there.

"Are you all right?" Endre inquired, his brows raised in concern as he looked up at Nora from between her legs, his thumbs hooked into the waistband of her panties.

"Y-yes," she lied, attempting to will her body to relax.

"Nora..." the word held the same question as his gaze. "I will not bite you," he assured her.

"Okay," she breathed out, closing her eyes and taking a deep breath. Was she really going to let a Vampire eat her out?

Endre slowly slid her panties down over her hips, her ass, her thighs, his fingers trailing over where the fabric whispered along her nerve-endings. When she was completely bare beneath him, he massaged his hands up her calves to her thighs, gently prying them apart to expose her most private place.

"I am not going to hurt you," he reassured, his breath blowing across her wetness with each word.

With the first swipe of his tongue over her wet folds, she was sure her eyes would roll into the back of her head. A pleased moan escaped from her lips and she wondered why she'd never let her ex do this before. It was pure heaven. Nora lost herself in the sensation of Endre's tongue bringing her closer to orgasm, until he slipped a finger inside her entrance.

Logic washed away all pleasure with a cold wave of reality. Was she really going to lose her virginity to a Vampire?

The moment he curled his finger upward, pressing against a spot she'd never been able to find herself, all concerns about what she was or wasn't going to do left her thoughts. Any doubts remaining were utterly washed away by the wave of her orgasm when it rushed over her.

CHAPTER TWENTY-THREE

"Oh God," *Nora* cried out, her body stiffening as she reached her climax.

Endre's lips curled into a satisfied smile as her body shivered with pleasure. He could not help himself, as he swiped his tongue through her folds one last time, earning a shuddering breath and a slight tremble of her body. She looked exactly as he imagined she would when she came—her cheeks rosy, mouth slightly agape, and her breasts rising and falling with each heaving breath she took. Heavy eyelids struggled to stay open as she watched him kiss a trail up her body. Nora was the picture-perfect definition of sated.

But he was not.

"Are you ready?" he murmured into her ear when he had traversed the length of her body, kissing every bit of skin he could reach on the journey northward.

Rigidity replaced the liquidity of her climax, and those heavy lids opened wide and fearful, all evidence of satisfaction erased from her body.

"What is it?" he asked, frowning down at the terror etched into her features.

"I..." she paused and swallowed, as if she searched for the right words. Her green gaze bounced between his eyes, unable to focus on one for more than a second. Silence hung in the air between them, her mouth silently agape. "Will it hurt?" she whispered.

Confused, he searched her expression for a clue, believing he had missed some part of the conversation. Did she believe he was to take her life *now*? Although she had experienced *la petite mort*, he had no intention of completing her transition at this time. "I am not going to hurt you," he reassured, smoothing a hand over her hair while he took in the abject terror of her expression.

"It's just that I've heard the first time hurts," she blurted out quickly, color rising in her cheeks when she attempted to look away.

"First time?" he questioned.

Then it dawned on him.

Nora was a virgin.

Silently, she nodded, her gaze roving over every object in the room which was not him.

A decidedly primal part of his being beat its chest in pride at the thought of being the first to sink inside her warmth. Then his mind stalled with the idea.

"Are you sure you want to do this?" He found it difficult to add the unspoken *with me, a monster* to the end of the question.

Her eyes hesitantly drifted to his, and he held her gaze for a few moments, attempting against hope to gauge her reaction, to glean an answer from her silence.

"Yes," she whispered, biting her lip and directing her gaze to the cuticles around her fingernails she picked at. "Can you just stop looking at me like that?" she implored, glancing up at him from beneath her eyebrows.

When he merely raised his eyebrows in question, afraid to vocalize his confusion, she let out a sigh.

"Like I'm some three-headed alien because I've never had sex before," she huffed. "You know, everyone makes this whole virginity thing out to be such a big deal, like it's got this invisible worth. I know it's uncommon for someone my age to still be a virgin."

Endre kept silent, unsure how to react. Unsure what to say.

"So, can we maybe just get this over with?"

"No," Endre said, sliding from the bed and taking a step back from the enticing woman lying on it.

Confusion knit her brows. "I thought you wanted to," she whispered, her expression halfway between sadness and anger.

"Nora, you are undoubtedly the most beautiful woman I have ever laid eyes on. But I refuse to rush through this. If you truly want this—with me—we will do this right. Intimacy is not something to 'just get it over with.' I would think, as someone who has made it this long in life without succumbing to the persuasion of men, you would not take this experience so lightly." Endre allowed his disapproval to bleed into his tone. Without a doubt, he wanted Nora in every way a man could, but he absolutely would not rush through something like this.

Propping herself up on her elbows, she fixed him with a furious expression.

It was all Endre could do to keep his eyes on hers and not watch the way her breasts rose and fell with each breath. "I will never understand women," he murmured to himself, allowing his gaze to roam over her body, even though he told himself he would not.

"And I'll never understand men," she huffed, the motion making her breasts bounce. "Every man I've ever met has been all about sex, and as soon as I'm finally willing to give it up, you don't want it."

"It is not a matter of want, *Elskling*."

"Then what is it?" Nora fixed him with a glare.

"It is about what the physical act represents. It is more than a satiation of the body's desires, it is a passionate connection between lovers. There is a reason it is referred to as 'making love.'"

Nora's eyebrows rose, as if in disbelief. "Why does it have to be about love? Why can't it just be about satisfying physical desires?"

"It is, for some. But not me," Endre explained, crossing his arms over his chest to indicate he held firm on his beliefs.

Skepticism crept into Nora's gaze. "You mean to tell me, in the nearly a thousand years you've been alive, that you've only 'made love' and never just fucked women?"

The word 'fuck' coming from her mouth grated on him for some reason. That was not what he wanted to be to her, just some quick fuck to rid herself of her virginity. The connection with her was what he sought. If he really did want a quick and dirty release, there were any number of women he could seduce and most he would not even need the aid of pheromones. "I prefer a deeper connection," he dodged, unwilling to entertain her desires for an unsatisfactory release. There were several Vampire women he had dalliances with over the years, but no humans, and nothing meaningful like he sought with Nora.

"And how many women over the course of a millennia have you found to connect with on such a deep level?" Her tone was mocking, the corners of her mouth turned up slightly in a smirk.

"Before you, there was only my wife," he divulged, cocking his head to the side as he awaited her reaction. He had thought for a moment about lying to her, but there was no point in keeping the truth from her.

Nora's eyes grew wide, then confused, the mocking challenge fading from them.

The mention of his late wife Ingrid thoroughly doused any flame of desire still remaining after the outset of this debate with Nora. "Perhaps it is best for you to get some sleep," he said with a deep sigh.

"I think you're right," she whispered, pulling the torn halves of her shirt together with a hard swallow.

Endre strode to the window, giving Nora his back and some privacy as she prepared herself for sleep. It was not how he had wanted things to end, but he hoped stopping what would surely end up a disaster would help him reclaim some sense of decency.

CHAPTER TWENTY-FOUR

With shaking hands, Nora pulled the torn shirt from her body and dropped it to the floor, leaving herself completely naked. But Endre didn't so much as glance back from where he stared out the window. That encounter hadn't gone at all how she'd expected. She'd thought for sure he'd ravage her like the Viking she knew he was, the moment she was bare beneath him. Finding he had such a hard boundary about sex was surprising. Learning he was married was downright shocking. That curious part of her wanted to pepper him with questions, but the thick silence and tension filling the room told her it would not be the best idea.

Exhaustion overwhelmed her, making the effort of finding intact clothes to wear monumental. Then there was the matter of her quivering limbs, still strung out from the heady orgasm he gave her. She supposed she should be thankful he had no qualms about giving her pleasure, because that climax was better than any she'd ever given herself.

Fuck it. Standing on wobbly legs beside the bed, she decided clothing was too much effort. And then there was the possibility that Endre would be in a giving mood when she woke. Keeping her eyes on his back, she slipped beneath the covers in nothing but her birthday suit.

It didn't take long for her mind to slip into one of Endre's memories.

Nora watched with detached fascination as she was enveloped in a short memory of Endre snatching a would-be rapist from the victim and spiriting him to the rooftop of a nearby building where he plunged his fangs into the criminal's neck, draining him slowly and painfully. Endre had his hand over the man's mouth to muffle his cries, but Nora sensed the pleasure Endre felt at the man's pain. The man died in agony, and Endre dropped the body in a nearby river. Nora guessed by the landmark buildings along the bank that it was the Seine. She assumed this was one of Endre's victims from the last several days due to the man's clothes. The scene faded to black, almost as if it were a scripted movie, just as she watched Endre plunge into the water after the man and weigh him down with a gigantic rock.

Nora tried to pull herself from her mind's prison, but the blood memories had other ideas. She emerged in Endre's body once again, this time during the night of some much older time, though it was difficult to pinpoint. The surrounding buildings were made of cob with thatched roofs, making Nora think of the Renaissance Festival back home. There seemed to be no chronological sense to the memories and it made things all the more disorienting. She never knew *when* she was looking at in these memories, which also meant she almost never knew *where*, either. This made her realize she didn't know much about where he came from or where he'd been, how he'd spent his life as a Vampire. Endre was clearly old, based upon the memory she experienced of when he was first turned, with savage-looking men in furs with great swords.

Endre stalked silently through the shadows of yet another memory, searching out prey. His footsteps made no sound on the cobblestones. More than once, he nodded to passersby and continued moving on. Nora was surprised he would bypass lone persons walking in the dead of night and wondered what he was waiting for. His head whipped around where he spied a man holding a dagger to the throat of another. A mugging in progress, Nora realized. Endre was on the perpetrator in an instant and snatched him into the shadows so fast, the thief's victim never even caught a glimpse of what saved him. Endre devoured his victim, but this time left the body lying in a dirty alleyway. As a warning, Nora surmised. The memory quickly moved on to where Endre found another criminal, and then another, snuffing out all of their lives.

After the fifth victim, shown in an icy, desolate wilderness wasteland, Nora was convinced of a pattern. He had only killed criminals in these memories. He was a vigilante killer who prowled in the shadows, using scum and vagabonds to quench his thirst. He was, in essence, one of the anti-heroes from her favorite movie genre. No, she was trying to justify his violence, trying to romanticize it. He'd still killed her classmates, her professor, and the cop back at the house. But if circumstances were different, if he hadn't been starved, if they had met him in a dark alleyway, would he have just passed them by? Would he have passed her by, too?

Nora cried out as she was forcefully ejected from the final memory of the sequence, almost like a physical shove as she awakened in her own body.

"Shhhh," Endre shushed in her ear, his arm wrapping tightly around her as he pulled her close. He whispered foreign words into her hair, his tone soothing as he brushed tender kisses along her neck.

The closeness of his body sent a shot of warmth through her, but as she pressed back into him, she found there was still a blanket between them. While she was in the buff beneath the covers, he was still clothed in his boxers on top of them. Despite the extra barrier, Nora arched her back into him, searching for the hard outline of his arousal. A soft moan sounded from her when she felt his hardness pressed against her back.

"Nora," he groaned, a note of warning in his tone.

The deep timbre of his voice and the way his hot breath fanned over the back of her neck set her blood on fire. "I want you," she whispered to him.

"You do not know what you are asking, *Elskling*. I am barely holding onto my control as it is," he growled, squeezing her breast in one hand.

"I do know," Nora insisted, reaching behind her to grab ahold of his stiff member.

"Gods," Endre cursed through clenched teeth. "I want more than a quick fuck. I want *you*. All of you," he warned.

Before that last memory, the thought of really giving herself to him would have terrified her. But now—she knew he wasn't quite the type of monster he led her to believe he was. He wasn't bloodthirsty and wild, he was discerning with his prey, or at least he had been before being buried for a century, and he was striving to regain that control. She'd already noticed a change in him.

"Please," she pleaded, pushing her breast further into his hand.

"You do not know what it does to me to hear you beg," he groaned, burying his face into her neck and nipping lightly.

A gasp sounded from her when he flipped her to her back, ripping the blanket from her. Completely exposed, she peered up at the Vampire hovering above her, his elbows planted beside her head. His normally ice-cold eyes heated as they roamed over her nudity.

"Gods, you are beautiful." Placing his weight on one forearm, he trailed fingers down the length of her torso, brushing his fingers teasingly at the juncture of her thighs.

When Nora gave a small moan, he swiped his fingers along her growing wetness, dipping a single digit inside her entrance. The slow slide of his finger coupled with his thumb at her clit elicited a gasp from her, which Endre swallowed when his mouth fused with hers. With agonizing slowness, he continued to explore her folds while he devoured her mouth.

"Please," Nora begged when his lips began to travel the length of her neck.

She could see it in his eyes, his resolve was cracking, it would only be a matter of time before he gave in to her pleas.

"You do not know what you do to me," he said, his breath shuddering in her ear.

Judging by the steely length of him, she had a pretty good idea. "I have an inkling," she replied just as breathlessly as she ran her hand along the bulge in the front of his pants.

Another groan sounded from him, clenching her core.

Climbing down her body, his hot breath washed over her skin.

Anticipation of his wicked tongue between her thighs again sent butterflies swirling in her belly.

Once again, he displayed his prowess, bringing her to a shuddering orgasm and transforming her into a molten pile of limbs. Nora was barely aware of Endre kissing along the inside of her thighs through the haze of endorphins.

"Satisfied?" he murmured against her flesh, gazing up at her from between her legs.

"Not even close," she told him with a lazy smile. "I want more. I want *you*."

Hunger flashed in his eyes as he rose to his feet and he pushed his boxers to the floor.

Nora's eyes widened when she took in the sight of his erection. Feeling it through his clothing was one thing, but seeing it was a whole other thing entirely.

There was no way that was fitting inside her.

A deep rumbling laugh shook Endre as he watched her shake her head. "What is the matter, lamb?"

"I don't think that's going to fit," she told him.

"Another time then." A grin pulled at the corner of his mouth as he slid into the bed beside her, covering his glorious body with the blanket.

"You're not getting off that easy," she said, frowning at him when she turned his way.

"I am not getting off at all," he pointed out.

"Endre," she sighed, running her hand down his naked chest. "I want to do this."

Indecision warred in his eyes. He watched her warily with furrowed brows when she leaned closer, pressing her lips to his. "I do not want you to regret this," he said, brushing her hair back from her face and cupping her cheek.

"I won't," she whispered, trailing her fingers over his taut abs to the v leading to his cock.

Endre sucked in a breath, his hips moving toward her exploring hand. A low groan sounded from him when she finally wrapped her hand around his length.

Slowly, Nora moved her hand up and down his length, taking immense pleasure in the expression of pure bliss on his face.

"Gods, Nora," he groaned, tipping his head back and closing his eyes.

"I need you, please?"

In a flurry of movement, his eyes flew open, and Nora found herself on her back once again. Endre's weight pressed her into the mattress, his hardness pressing into her belly. A gasp came from her when she caught sight of the wild look in his eyes.

"There is no going back," he warned, easing his body up, and slipping his hardness to rest against her entrance. "Are you sure you want this?"

"Yes," she assured him, meeting his intense gaze.

With agonizing slowness, he eased his hardness inside her.

Mouth agape, she stared into his eyes while her body adjusted to the sensation of feeling so full.

He continued to hold her gaze as he eased forward, breaching her virginity.

A stinging sensation accompanied the loss of her virginity and Nora sucked in a startled breath. "I'm okay," she reassured when Endre began to withdraw from her, his brows furrowed with concern.

Stilling his movements, he lowered his lips to hers. "Do you want me to stop?"

"No," Nora protested, her voice too loud in the stillness of the room. "No."

With the same careful composure, Endre continued to move within her. Each drag of his desire through her channel sent a wave of pleasure through her. When he picked up his pace, she couldn't take anymore and rubbed the bundle of nerves between her thighs.

Pushing her hand aside, Endre resumed her movement, matching the tempo of his thrusts to his fingers. Pressure built deep in her core, waiting to be unleashed.

"Endre," she called breathlessly.

Endre's mouth met hers in a frantic clash of lips, tongues and teeth. Sharp teeth. The bite of fangs on her overly sensitive lip didn't break her from the lust-induced haze, even as the wave of her orgasm crashed over her

Somewhere nearby, Endre groaned long and low, his lips now brushing along the side of her neck, his fangs dragging along the sensitive skin, but not biting.

"Do it," she whispered, twining her hand into the strands of her hair to keep him there.

Just as he bit into her neck, he flicked his thumb over her clit, sending another climax crashing over her. When the high finally receded, it left her raw and shaking—her hearing muffled and her vision blurred.

"Holy wow," she gasped, blinking to clear the fuzziness from her eyes. "That was intense."

Endre ran his tongue along her throat one more time, before rolling to the side, breathing hard, but he nodded his assent.

Staring at the ceiling, Nora hovered in her euphoric daze, feeling the manic stuttering of her heart and willing her breathing to slow.

As the chemicals released in her brain with her orgasm began to recede, she was left with the question—now what? They'd taken their twisted companionship to a new level, and having crossed that line, there was no going back.

I'm not a virgin anymore. At least she wouldn't die having never had sex. It was just too bad she didn't learn until now what she'd been missing out on. However, she had a sneaking suspicion that things would have been leagues different if it had been anyone other than Endre.

The mattress shifted beneath her, drawing her attention to where Endre stood beside the bed, watching her curiously.

"How do you feel?" he asked, tenderly brushing a tendril of hair from her forehead.

"Tired," Nora whispered, his assessing gaze ratcheting her anxiety up to unprecedented levels.

With a nod, Endre scooped her naked body into his arms, lifting her from the rumpled sheets.

A startled yelp sounded from Nora before she could gather her words. "What are you doing?" she questioned as he carried her to the bathroom.

"Taking care of you," he stated simply when he set her atop vanity beside the sink.

Speechless, Nora observed him run a washcloth under the faucet, steam rising from the water. Her brain had a difficult time processing what was happening when he wiped between her thighs, cleaning away the mixture of his seed and the traces of blood from her broken hymen.

Am I in shock? Nora wondered when she couldn't find the words to protest the intimate care he provided. Shock seemed most likely. She *did* just lose her virginity to a Vampire. And not just any Vampire, but one who had been holding her captive for the last several days. Emotions continued to evade her when Endre carried her back to the bed and wrapped his body around hers.

CHAPTER TWENTY-FIVE

The steady beat of his heart against her back was more soothing than it should be. Somehow, after everything she'd been through, she felt *safe* in his arms. She couldn't name what was happening between them—the shift they'd made from captor and captive to lovers. Others would probably tell her she was experiencing Stockholm Syndrome, but it was more than that. It had to be. There was this connection she couldn't shake, like he knew her better than anyone else. And yet, she knew so little about him.

"I can practically hear the gears turning in that mind of yours, *Elskling*," Endre's low voice rumbled into her ear.

A thrilling shiver ran through her body with the vibrations at her back.

"Where are you from?" Nora asked into the darkness.

"Where, or when?" Endre responded, nuzzling along her neck.

"Both."

"I suppose there is no harm in telling. Who I was before this life is not who I am now. I was born near the Oslo Fjord in Vestfold in Norway. I do not know that I can say the exact year, sometime around 840 AD, near the same time King Fairhair, the first king of a united Norway was born."

"So, you're an 1175-year-old Viking?" Nora wasn't sure why the revelation surprised her. There were plenty of clues in the memories she'd seen that most definitely indicated he had lived in the distant past.

"Now a Vampire. I was a warrior. I was part of Harald Fairhair's horde, amassed to win the challenge his lady interest, Gyda, flung at him. Do you know the story?"

"No, I don't think so," Nora confessed, wracking her brain for any stories her grandmother may have told her of King Fairhair. No recollections came to mind. Grandmother had spoken of Fairhair once or twice, but Nora had always assumed from the name that he was a figure more of myth than history.

"Fairhair was a young king, but ambitious. He was taken with a rival king's daughter, Gyda, and sent his men to retrieve her so he could claim her as a concubine. But when his men reached her, she refused to be treated so lowly."

"Good for her," Nora snorted.

"She sent word back to the king that she had no intention of becoming his concubine, but she would consider being his rightful bride if only his kingdom were larger—spanning the whole of Norway. King Harald took her challenge and set about conquering all of Norway to win her approval," Endre continued on, as if he hadn't noted her interruption.

"Is that the war where you died? Are these scars from then?" Nora inquired, brushing her hand along an upraised mark on his forearm.

"Yes, it was the final battle at Hafrsfjord that my first life ended and my second began. As a human, I did not live to see the end of that war or the uniting of the kingdom. Though I did learn after I was forced from my homeland that Gyda's father's forces fell and she became one of King Fairhair's wives. The scars are from before I was reborn. I was still learning when I got this one," he recounted, moving her hand along a long-faded scar on his bicep. "So much bloodshed all for the sake of a woman. I should learn from the lessons of history and remember that your sex is nothing but trouble." A light chuckle shook his frame behind her.

"Don't forget you're the one who dragged me into all of this. I didn't ask for any of it," Nora responded bitterly.

"I know it," he said with an exasperated sigh. "But perhaps some good will come of it yet, and I can give you the second chance you deserve."

"We both know that's a long shot," Nora murmured, pulling in a deep breath to quell the oncoming tears.

"If not as a human, then as an immortal until the cure."

The hope in his voice formed a pit in her stomach. He'd convinced her before with the utmost conviction he was going to get this cure right. The hope spelled uncertainty to her ears.

"I will atone for my sins. I can only hope for redemption."

There was the conviction.

"Is that why you mostly feed from criminals? To seek redemption and atonement?" Nora ventured. She sincerely wanted to know now if she had imagined the pattern in his victims in the last memory she'd experienced.

"To ease the burdens of my heart and mind, yes, I try to keep to preying off those who prey on others," he acknowledged, nodding slowly. "But the cure is where I believe my salvation lies. I began to study blood and unlock the secrets to the mysterious hold it has over my kind. I started my research looking for a way to ease the thirst so we did not have to prey on humans. That morphed into something more. I wanted to find a cure for Vampirism as a whole, to completely reverse this cursed existence. But soon, I found once the transition is complete, it is no longer a matter of the blood, but genetics. I never concluded my research, but I believe I know how it can be done. I had plenty of time to think on it," Endre replied, his tone rougher and darker when he spoke of his time being buried.

"Because you were imprisoned?" she guessed, relaxing into him a little.

"Yes," he replied simply.

"Is *that* why they buried you? Your research, I mean?" Nora inquired, her curiosity rearing its ugly head again. She didn't know if she really wanted to know, but she had to admit this new side of him was fascinating, and it revealed more of the humanness she had felt was trapped beneath the driving Vampire need for blood.

"Essentially, yes. There are those amongst us who no longer view Vampires as a mutation of the human species but as an entirely separate and superior species. They do not believe as I do, that we should work to curb our appetites and work toward finding alternative means of survival. One such person is the reason I was buried for nine decades. I told Lorenzo and one other man about my research. Lorenzo then killed this other man I had confided in and framed me for the murder then had me imprisoned for his crime. To kill another Vampire is a grievous offense, yet the punishment for such a crime cannot be death at the hands of another Vampire because it would then condemn the executioner as well. You can see how that chain of logic would lead to our extinction. Instead, the punishment was for the accused to endure death naturally as well as slow and agonizing. The only 'natural' death a Vampire can suffer is starvation. It is a slow and painful process that takes centuries. In the days of more superstitious and less educated times, Vampires were buried as punishment until they confessed to their crimes, their confession being their own demise or escape. It was thought if a Vampire rose from his grave, he was innocent of his accused crimes and allowed to continue to live out his second life in peace."

Nora listened, awed by his words.

"I had hoped some of those old laws still prevailed and since I had risen, I would be allowed my freedom and pardon from the crimes I was accused of. It would seem these modern Vampires have moved away from The Council's ways. My sources tell me Lorenzo has proclaimed himself ruler here in France and has enacted his own set of laws," Endre lectured, his tone hard again.

"That's pretty messed up." Nora shivered when flashes of his memories from underground passed through her brain.

"It is quite archaic, I admit. Those practices have been upheld in the name of 'tradition,' though many protest their barbarism. Unfortunately for me, Lorenzo merely preyed on the Vampire collective's desire to uphold such practices to remove me from his schemes." Endre placed a kiss on her neck.

"I can understand why you want revenge. I saw the memories. Are you sure leaving here will give you the closure you need to make things right?" She tilted her neck to give him better access to trail his sinful lips down the sensitive skin of her neck.

"No, it will not provide me with closure, especially since he will surely come after us, now that he knows I am above the earth again. He expects me to come for him, but if I do not, he will surely hunt for me. I am a threat to everything he holds dear and the longer the span of time between our confrontation, the longer he will be looking over his shoulder and waiting. He will no doubt act quickly as a matter of strategy."

"I imagine it's difficult to build an evil Vampire empire if you're constantly looking over your shoulder for your arch nemesis," Nora commented with a yawn, exhaustion and the warmth of his body around hers pulling her eyelids closed.

Endre snorted behind her. "Arch nemesis, I like that. But enough talk." Leaning forward, he peered at the clock on the nightstand. "We should be leaving."

"I don't know that I can stay awake another minute, let alone be alert enough for a stealthy escape," Nora admitted.

"I wish we could stay longer," Endre murmured against her skin between kisses down the length of her neck.

"Why can't we?" she groaned, burying her head in the pillow. Once they left this hotel room, it was back to constant peril. At least here, with her head buried in down feathers, she could pretend they were two lovers on a romantic getaway in Paris.

"Lorenzo should already be here by now. I am surprised he is not, although I can imagine he is waiting for us to leave this establishment." A sigh. "I should not have indulged my baser needs," he chided himself. "Now it will be much more difficult to escape intact." Rising from the bed, he strode across the room to their packed luggage awaiting their departure.

Nora's gaze followed his nude form, admiring the muscles stretching and flexing with each step. A shuddering breath left her, sending warmth straight to her core.

"Unfortunately, we do not have time for that again," he told her with a mischievous wink over his shoulder.

Damn those Vampire senses, she'd never be able to hide when she was horny. "Where are we going?" she asked in an attempt to direct her thoughts away from the images of him thrusting into her.

"Away from France, I do not know where yet. Once we are far enough from Lorenzo's clutches, I will be able to determine the best location to set up a lab where I can begin work on a cure for you."

"For me?" Nora pushed herself to sitting, the blissful cloud melting away and leaving behind suspicion. "What do you mean? You said you weren't going to turn me."

"I will not." A determined glint lit his eye and his jaw clenched tight.

"Then what do you mean?" she demanded, narrowing her eyes as she searched his face. "What aren't you telling me?"

His expression grew pained as he drew in a deep breath, then hung his head. "I had hoped we would not have this conversation. I had hoped I could find a cure before..."

Nora watched him rub his hands over his face, waiting for him to continue. He didn't. "Before what?" she whispered. "It's already happening, isn't it? I'm already turning into a Vampire."

Endre shook his head. "No, not that. You are dying."

"I-I don't understand?" she managed to choke out around the lump in her throat. Clutching the rumpled sheet, she drew it around her, as if it could protect her from whatever words came out of the Vampire's mouth.

Cocking his head to the side, his eyes roamed over her face, his brows pinched together. "You sincerely do not know the extent of your illness, do you?"

All Nora could do was stare at him with wide eyes, fear snatching any words she might have directly from her brain.

"There is a cancer in your blood," he explained. "I could taste it the first time I drank from you."

"Wait," she paused for a moment, her brain coming back on line. "Cancer? No. You're wrong," she protested, but a voice in the back of her mind reminded her of the vials of blood pending results at the campus clinic. They had been just a precaution, a way to get her mother and Chloe off her back about feeling so tired.

"It is progressing quickly. Even the healing capabilities of my blood have only been able to slow the attack by minuscule amounts. It is in the very marrow of your bones."

"No." Shaking her head, she wiped at the wetness trailing down her cheeks. "I was fine. Just a little tired."

"Nora," Endre stepped toward her.

"You did this!" she accused, rising from the bed with the sheet still clutched around her. "I was fine until you came along. Until you *kidnapped* me and *killed* everyone around me."

"Were you?" he questioned, his tone turned icy as he crossed his arms and stared dispassionately at her from across the room. "You were fine, but you had all those tests run at the clinic on campus?"

"How did you...?"

"Your blood holds memories as well. I saw when they took vial after vial of blood."

Leukemia, that was the word that she'd been struggling to dig up from the depths of her memories. There was a boy in her class in third grade who'd had it, so the teacher taught them about it. He didn't make it and they named a park after him. Nora had a feeling no one would be naming any parks after her when she died. It made a sick sort of sense now, though—the soreness emanating from her very bones, the extreme exhaustion. But then again, he could be wrong.

He could be lying.

"You're telling me I have Leukemia, and you were what? Going to just concoct a cure for something that no one else has been able to come up with before?" A mirthless laugh escaped her.

"That was my initial plan."

"Right." Nora nodded, attempting to ignore the tears prickling behind her eyes.

"I can see you are having trouble believing me. What must I do to convince you I speak the truth?"

"It's certainly far-fetched, but I suppose if anyone can detect a problem with a person's blood, a Vampire could." A shudder ran through her, she was so cold.

"It is more than that. A mere Vampire can taste anomalies in the blood, but one familiar with such anomalies can identify them. When you relived my memories, you saw when I was first imprisoned beneath the ground, correct?"

"Yes." Nora shuddered at the vision of the memory as it came to mind.

"How much of that memory did you experience? Did you happen to see the bit where

Lorenzo confessed his treachery before the final nail in the coffin, so to speak?"

Furrowing her brow, Nora attempted to recall the grisly scene.

"He opposed my research to develop a cure for Vampirism. Before I was imprisoned, I was a hematologist."

"You were a blood doctor?" Nora gaped. "Oh, the irony."

"There was nothing ironic about it," Endre insisted. "I worked tirelessly to cure my kind of the Vampire condition. I had intended to continue that research the moment I dispatched Lorenzo. But now I have another purpose to fulfill first."

Nora slumped back to the edge of the bed, holding her head in her hands. He'd been telling her all along she was going to die. Who knew he'd been telling the truth that entire time? Here, she thought he'd been referring to his intent to kill her, when really it was the information he withheld and the misguided notion he could magically cure something others had been working at for over a hundred years. "You've been buried for a century and no one has cured Leukemia in that time."

"That will not stop me from trying," he insisted, steel in his tone.

"And what happens when you fail? I die."

Endre shook his head, his gaze solemn as he locked eyes with her. "No, not death."

Silence hung heavy between them, then it dawned on her what he meant. "No, I don't want that." Nora shook her head violently from side to side. "You keep telling me how horrible it is to be a Vampire, why would you do that to me?"

"The matter is out of my hands at this point." He held his hands up in a gesture of helplessness.

"What the fuck is that supposed to mean?" she railed, her stomach roiling with all the tension.

"By my estimates, even if I continue to feed you my blood, the cancer will overtake your body in a matter of weeks and you will die. With my blood in your system. If I discontinue feeding you my blood, the degeneration rate would be even faster, and you would still die with my blood in your system."

"Either way, I'm fucked," Nora whispered, more to herself than the Vampire in the room.

Endre shook his head. "No."

Nora scoffed and ran her hands over her face to hide the tears now tracking down her cheeks.

"We will leave here immediately. I will set up a lab, and either I cure you of your Leukemia before time runs out, or I cure us both of Vampirism after you have completed the transition," he professed without an ounce of doubt.

"Those are both pretty fucking tall orders, Endre," she reminded him with a scowl as she yanked the tail of the sheet to wrap it to further conceal her body. Dashing the tears from her cheeks, she attempted to quell the flow while her mind churned with the consequences of her new reality. She was going to die. And when she died, she would turn into a Vampire. It was one of those things just about every girl fantasized about when reading popular Vampire novels—that a sexy as sin immortal would enter their lives and offer everlasting life. The notion was far more romantic than the reality of it though. Just the thought of drinking blood night after night to stay alive turned her stomach, especially considering the source of that sustenance.

She was turning into a monster.

CHAPTER TWENTY-SIX

Nora's gaze had taken on a far-away quality, her thoughts obviously turning inward as her mind struggled to make sense of the information Endre had just given her. The conversation had not gone as he had hoped. Gods, the very idea of how to tell her what was in store for her had plagued him for days, but he would have preferred to wait until they were far away from Lorenzo's dominion before breaking such devastating news.

Silence seeped into the empty spaces of the room, filling where words could not, slowly choking Endre and any hope he had of convincing Nora that all hope was not lost. "Nora?" he managed to force the word out, dispelling the silence like the sun scattering the night.

She remained mute, her eyes unfocused as she continued to stare at a point somewhere in a plane beyond his sight.

Before his very eyes, his light, his Eleanora, slipped toward the inky pit of despair. It was a desolate, unpleasant place, a space he had occupied on more than one occasion in his long life. Once a mind wandered into that dark abyss, the only certainty in escape was that a piece of you would always remain. With each step forward, every hostile thought clung to the skin like briars, tearing at the flesh and draining away the very will to leave. Endre knew from experience it took great will and determination to climb from the chasm, there were some who never emerged alive. Nora would, of that he was confident, because she had him to pull her to safety when her steps faltered.

"*Elskling*," Endre coaxed, framing Nora's face in his hands, turning her gaze from the empty walls to his eyes. "You need to dress and we will leave. I will make this right, I promise." A hard knot formed in his stomach at his last words, an iron-clad declaration that he would make her life worth living.

Nora ran her hands over her face, her features a mask of deceptive calm. It was her eyes which gave her away, though. They took on a glassy sheen of tears barely held back. "Okay," she told him, nodding resolutely, her throat bobbing as she swallowed. "Let's get out of here so we can figure this out."

Relief flooded Endre. She was not completely herself and he imagined it would be awhile before she would be, but at least she was interacting with him.

Taking a suitcase in each hand, he pulled them to the door and waited for Nora to dress and gather the last of her belongings and join him.

Her movements were slow, but methodical as she gave the room one more look to ensure nothing was left behind.

"I believe our best mode of transportation would be the train," he commented when she finally joined him at the door, pulling it closed behind them.

"Where are we going?" she asked her voice low and melancholy.

"Italy."

The movement was barely perceptible, but the slight twitch of her eyebrow upward projected her doubts about his plan as clearly as if she had scoffed at him.

"My primary objective is to remove us from such close proximity to Lorenzo. Once we are safe outside his reach, I can begin work," Endre explained as he punched the down button on the wall of the elevator bank.

Nodding, Nora stepped into the car, her gaze fixed on the floor between her feet.

"*Elskling,*" he prodded, placing a finger beneath her chin to lift her gaze to his. "I will not fail you."

"I believe you'll try," she replied with a deep sigh. "But it's a long shot, isn't it?"

A sliver of doubt leeched into the cracks of his determination, bringing with it a moment of hesitation Nora identified immediately. "It will take me some time," he admitted. "But it is not impossible," he added when tears welled in her eyes again.

"I'll try to be patient. It'll be hard, though," she admitted with a wan, watery smile.

The utter despair in every molecule of her being pulled at his heartstrings, sending a pang through his chest. Failing was not an option, seeing Nora like this until his goal was accomplished would be motivation enough. "I *will not* fail you," he repeated.

Nora's gaze drifted to her feet once more.

Keeping his gentle grip on her chin, Endre dipped his head to meet her eyes. "That is a promise," he pronounced, sealing the proclamation with the brush of his lips against hers.

Her entire body went rigid for a fraction of a moment before her mouth moved against his, her hand coming to rest on his chest, directly over his heart.

The slight lurch of the elevator car coupled with the slide of the doors opening interrupted the tender moment. Nora blinked up at him, her eyes dazed, but seemed more herself than he had seen in her since breaking the news of her dismal future.

Endre cursed the timing of the contraption and with a sigh took hold of the suitcases once more, wheeling them into the lobby.

"Ah, you're finally packed up," a black-clad man observed as he stepped into view, along with another half dozen Vampires. "Come with us, Lorenzo is expecting you."

CHAPTER TWENTY-SEVEN

Endre's first instinct was to fight. It could not be helped, his Viking blood sang at the opportunity for a skirmish. Releasing the luggage, he quickly pushed Nora behind him and assumed a defensive stance, his hand darting to the firearm tucked at his back.

"I wouldn't do that if I were you," the Vampire before him warned, brandishing his own gun, taking aim at Nora.

Defeat coursed through Endre, cold and biting. Even with as fast as he was, by the time he drew the gun and squeezed off a round, the other Vampire's bullet would already be lodged somewhere in Nora's body. And if this Vampire happened to miss, the probability of the six others doing the same was infinitesimally small.

With a deep inhale, Endre rose to his full height, holding his hands up in surrender.

"That's what I thought." Lorenzo's henchman chortled with a smirk. "Bind him," he directed, waving his gun in Endre's direction.

Three of the entourage moved forward and Endre's muscles tensed once again. Though his mind knew any attempt to fight would only put Nora in danger, he found it difficult to separate the logic from the instincts and muscle memory of his body.

With great reluctance, he placed his fisted hands together, proffering them to his captors. Taking deep breaths, he fought against the tsunami of adrenaline flooding his system. The rush of his blood in his own ears could not drown out the sound of Nora's frantic heartbeats, her terror audible.

"Behind your back," the lead Vampire ordered, motioning for Endre to turn.

Slowly, Endre pivoted so his back was to his enemy and he had a heart-wrenching view of Nora's wide, frightened eyes. The sight of her wiped all thoughts of compliance from his mind.

In the span of a second, he pushed Nora to the floor with one hand, the other drawing the pistol from where it rested at his lower back and fired off a volley of well-aimed shots at Lorenzo's entourage. Two Vampires dropped to the floor, blood pouring from head wounds. A third gasped and dropped to his knees when a bullet grazed his heart. But a second was all it took for the henchmen to regain their composure and retaliate.

"Take him alive!" the leader shouted amidst the gunshots.

Nora screamed from somewhere behind Endre, but his focus was on the bullets impacting his body. The remaining four Vampires emptied their clips into him, deliberately missing fatal targets of his head and heart. Weakly, he hefted a mangled arm in an attempt to take out just one more of the bastards, but the damage was too extensive. His gun clattered against the marble tile of the foyer as it slipped from his blood-slickened hand.

"Endre!" Nora cried, her voice sounding as if it came from beneath some far-off ocean.

Black swarmed the edges of his vision, his body swaying as blood poured from countless wounds. A sickening thud sounded when his knees met marble as his legs gave out beneath him. Endre's head lolled to the side, blood seeping from the corners of his mouth, as he fought to remain conscious.

"I'm going to enjoy watching Lorenzo flay your flesh from your bones," the leader of Lorenzo's henchmen spat. Drawing his arm back with a sneer, his fist connected with the side of Endre's face.

With a groan, Endre crumpled to the ground, his face colliding with the cold marble made wet by his own blood. The angry faces of the Vampires swam in his failing vision as the four of them drove him closer to unconsciousness with their fists.

"Endre!"

Nora's scream was the last thing to pierce through the coming darkness before the world went black.

CHAPTER TWENTY-EIGHT

"Endre!" Nora screamed, scrambling across the marble foyer to where four Vampires kicked the shit out of him.

The malevolent glare of one of the Vampires turned to her.

"Grab her," the head Vampire ordered in his thick accent, nodding toward Nora before placing one last kick to Endre's ribs. "Asshole," he spat.

There was no time to react before one of the Vampires gripped her arm tightly and hauled her to her feet. Letting out a hiss of pain, she stumbled to stay upright.

"Do you want me to bind her?" her captor asked, eying her critically.

The leader of the contingent examined her closely, his face in her personal bubble more than she would have liked as he inhaled her scent deeply. "No need, her body is weak with sickness. But make sure you keep a close eye on her. You two," he addressed the remaining Vampires, pointing at them. "Bind him and let's get going."

Without a moment's hesitation, the two Vampires roughly rolled Endre to his front and wrenched his arms behind his back to secure them. He let out a low groan, but they paid him no mind.

Nora let out a small sigh of relief when his pained sounds proved he was still alive. Though for how much longer, she could only guess.

Abrupt yanking on her arm brought Nora's attention away from the bloodied sight of Endre and back to the Vampire leaving bruises on her upper arm as he dragged her through the lobby. A soft cry of surprise escaped her when she caught sight of the front desk clerk sprawled on the floor, her limbs contorted at unnatural angles, and her eyes left open to stare lifelessly at the ceiling. The floor surrounding the body was slick with blood, the sight of such wanton violence turning her stomach. Bile rose into throat, burning a path in its wake, but she took deep breaths to keep from vomiting.

"If you vomit on me, human, I will kill you where you stand. Ordered to take you alive or not," her captor threatened.

Swallowing thickly, she was able to stave off the urge to heave. Barely.

A chuckle sounded from the leader as he matched pace with Nora. "Not feeling well?"

Narrowing her eyes, she glared at the Vampire with as much hatred as she could put into her expression.

"I can see why the traitor took a liking to you." He ran his tongue along the edge of his teeth as he surveyed her. "There's a bit of fire in you. I'm curious to see what Lorenzo has in store for you. If he doesn't want you as a pet of his own, I'll gladly keep you."

The thought of Lorenzo or any man other than Endre touching her struck her first with fear, then with rage. She was not a docile pet to be leashed and brought to heel. The saliva pooling in her mouth came in handy when she spat it in the Vampire's face with a sneer. "Nobody's keeping me."

Violent intent flashed across the Vampire's face, immediately turning his expression from mocking to furious. "You forget your place, *human,*" he growled, wiping his fingers across his cheekbone to collect the spittle. He glanced down at the wetness with profound distaste before his gaze slowly slid up to meet her eyes.

A spark of terror flashed through her. *What the hell am I doing antagonizing Vampires?*

"You'll learn pretty fucking quickly, if you don't die first," the leader threatened before his fist connected with her face.

Nora let out a cry of agony as white lights burst behind her eye with the impact.

"That's just a taste of what's to come," he warned, grabbing a fistful of her hair and hissing the words into her ear. "Let's move, he's expecting us," he ground out to the rest of his entourage.

The journey through the streets to Lorenzo's lair was a blur to Nora. Her vision was hazy and her head pounded fiercely from the Vampire's blow. At one point, the assailant holding her got fed up with her stumbling and simply threw her over his shoulder. The rhythmic bumping of her skull against his back sent the pounding in her head to excruciating levels.

When the air changed, Nora managed to open her eyes, finding herself still hanging upside down against a Vampire's back, but now they were no longer trudging through the streets. The inside of a building greeted her curious glance, the walls appearing to have been cut from stone. The view of the lobby was brief and quickly cut off by the darkened walls of a stairwell.

Blackness swallowed the group of them. The sounds of the party's scuffling footsteps across stone steps filled the stifling silence of the dark, though they were heavy and muffled as if insulated by the black surrounding them.

A person could go mad in a place like this and Nora was thankful they were passing through, rather than staying awhile. Although, the descent seemed to take hours until they reached the bottom at last and the Vampire carrying her propped her onto her feet.

CHAPTER TWENTY-NINE

Nora felt very much like the lamb being led to the slaughter as rough hands pushed her into what was more a cavern than a room. She gazed around in wonder at the high ceilings of roughly-hewn rock and the walls lit by flickering torches. It looked like something straight out of a novel, exactly the place one would expect to find a nest of Vampires.

At the front of the room, there was a stone dais with a single ornate chair atop it—a throne, she realized, with black banners emblazoned with a single blood-red fleur-de-lis hanging behind it. A tall man with raven black hair slicked back from his forehead and hawk-like features sat in the throne with one ankle crossed over his knee. He lounged with subtle grace, one arm draped across the upholstered armrest, the elbow of the other perched on the rich brocade with his chin resting upon his hand. His body looked at ease, but Nora could see the tension in his dark eyes. The man who sat atop the throne was none other than Lorenzo himself; she recognized him immediately from Endre's memory of his burial.

The Vampires left Nora a few feet from the dais and moved to the outskirts of the room, hidden once again in shadows where the light of the torches didn't reach. She could see others moving along the perimeter of illumination out of the corner of her eyes and got the impression of sharks circling when they smelled blood in the water.

"It would seem I underestimated you, dear friend," Lorenzo spoke, his gaze looking past Nora to a spot behind her.

Nora turned to look at Endre behind her, but as soon as she pivoted, Lorenzo stood before her, moving faster than she could even fathom. A sharp gasp left her when he filled her line of sight instead of Endre, as she'd expected.

"Friend?" Endre rasped out, his voice rough and filled with rage.

"Still angry about our little spat, are you? That was a lifetime ago," Lorenzo dismissed, his dark eyes focused on Nora's while he continued to speak to Endre.

Cold spread through Nora merely from the prolonged gaze into the dark pits of this villain's eyes. Endre was a Vampire and certainly, no saint, but

Lorenzo was something entirely different. Unspeakable evil lived inside this corpse of a man, not a shred of humanity remained.

"You left me buried for nearly a century for *your* crimes," Endre growled, his volume rising, echoing his voice off the stone walls. "Angry does not even begin to cover it."

"Come now, what is a century to us? But a few grains of sand in the hourglass. Let us look at this as water under the bridge, shall we?" Lorenzo assuaged with a deep chuckle.

Nora tried not to let her confusion show. Why all the small talk? If Lorenzo wanted them dead, his minions could have killed them back at the hotel. What was the point in bringing them here, unless his plans were more sinister than merely granting them death?

"You lit that bridge aflame when you slit my throat and buried me for your crimes. I pray those fires light your way to Hel." Endre sneered at him.

"Hell, that's rich." Lorenzo let out a hearty laugh. "You were always so dramatic. There is no need for theatrics and such animosity. Bygones and all that."

A smile that turned Nora's stomach curled up the corners of the Vampire's mouth.

"I have a proposition for you," Lorenzo continued, the ghoulish smile still gracing his lips. "A business proposal, as it were."

So that was it, he hadn't killed them because he wanted something from Endre.

"Fuck you and your proposal!" Endre spat.

A deep sigh came from Lorenzo. "I had hoped we could do this civilly. It seems I'll have to resort to more... drastic persuasion techniques." His eyes raked over Nora, settling on the pulse hammering in her neck.

"If you so much as touch her—" Endre ground out.

"You'll what?" Lorenzo said, his gaze whipping to Endre as he grabbed Nora, capturing her body in front of him so she faced Endre. "I have a dozen guards who will end your life at the snap of my fingers. Do not presume, for even a second that you have any power here. This is *my* domain. I tried to be gracious and give you a choice before it came to this."

Lorenzo's words came out in hot puffs of air against Nora's neck, but each word chilled her to the bone. There was no way to know what was in store for her, not really, but she could sure guess it wasn't going to be pleasant. A whimper escaped her when he tightened the arm holding tight across her belly.

Endre's blood-covered face was contorted in an expression equal parts agony and fury, a terrifying sight to behold.

"Humans make such poor pets, don't you think? So delicate and short-lived. She is beautiful," Lorenzo murmured, running his nose along the length of her neck. "Perhaps I'll keep her for myself."

Tremors wracked Nora's body and the sound of Endre's feral growls sent goosebumps racing across her flesh.

"It's a shame you didn't turn her. Why *haven't* you turned her?" Lorenzo inquired, his tone taking on a note of genuine curiosity. "I haven't been able to figure that out. No matter, she'd make a wonderful addition to my flock. Don't you think?

No sooner had the taunt left Lorenzo's lips than Endre lurched forward against the bonds still held by his captors, filling the cavernous room with snarls of frustration and the metallic clinking of chains. "She will never be one of your vultures," Endre seethed with a growl.

"Ahh, I see we have a misunderstanding. You speak of birds and I speak of sheep. We keep a store of them now, you know, humans to feed from. It gets less messy than hunting in the streets. Although, a lion is a lion and needs to hunt, so we do allow that from time to time." Lorenzo mused, inspecting Nora closely, as if she were livestock up for auction. "It is a pity you didn't turn her when you had the chance. Why hasn't he turned you?" he directed the question to her, burying his face in her hair and inhaling deeply. "What was it, Endre? Let me guess, you wanted to spare her the agony of immortality?" Lorenzo's tone was mocking, though it rang with truth. "You'd spare her your imagined pain, and yet you wouldn't do her the service of ending her miserable mortal life before illness claimed her? It must be love."

Endre's eyes narrowed on Lorenzo, his body still held at bay by the chains clutched in his guards' hands. "Make your proposal and be done with it."

"See, there, I knew you could be reasonable," the villain answered, his voice smug. "I want us to work together on your cure."

Suspicion filled Endre's expression, a furrow forming between his brows. "Why? You were not terribly keen on the idea of a cure when we spoke of it last."

"Call it an investment," Lorenzo replied with a nonchalant shrug. "I have a buyer who will pay handsomely for such a thing. Think of it. I could provide you with nearly unlimited resources. You could accomplish your life-long dream of living out your remaining days as a fragile human again."

"Who is the buyer?" Endre pressed.

"Leave the business dealings to me, hm?" Lorenzo answered with a condescending sigh.

"I will not have you use my good intentions as a weapon," Endre protested, shaking his head slowly, his gaze meeting Nora's.

"Your input isn't part of the deal. You work on the cure and you and your human pet live happily ever after—as long as her disease allows. You have no leverage here," Lorenzo reminded them both, nuzzling along Nora's neck.

"I must if you are still attempting to negotiate," Endre said.

"Yet another misunderstanding. This isn't a negotiation. You will help me, one way or another. Allowing your human to live is merely a courtesy because I was in a good mood." Lorenzo clasped a hand around Nora's throat in demonstration.

A pitiful whimper sounded from Nora through the tightening of her throat. Cold sweat prickled along her skin as panic began to work its way into her mind.

"I'm not in a good mood anymore," Lorenzo stated, pulling a dagger from his hip and flashing it for both Nora and Endre to see. Nora recognized it as the dagger he'd used to cut across Endre's throat in one of the blood memories she'd relived.

"If you harm her—" Endre shouted, his chains clinking as he struggled against them, his wide eyes shining with a manic light.

"Your threats are empty here. How many times must I remind you how little power you hold? It seems my point hasn't come across yet. My patience is at an end. Perhaps this will illustrate my point."

The cold bite of metal followed by unspeakable pain tore across Nora's throat as Lorenzo drew his blade through her flesh. Warm liquid spilled from the gaping wound, choking off her screams. Pure and utter agony overwhelmed her every sense, her arms struggling against Lorenzo's hold to stanch the flow of blood.

"Say goodbye to your pet, Endre. Before I rend your head from your neck, I want you to watch her die, knowing it is your fault. It was your refusal to perform one simple task which brought us to this point," Lorenzo whispered, holding Nora fast, despite her struggling and convulsing.

The pain all at once became too overwhelming, her brain unable to handle the massive overload of sensation. Numbness crept into every crevice of her being and Nora watched with disoriented detachment as

Endre's face contorted with rage, a scream of fury leaving his lips as he ripped the chains free from his captors and rushed toward where Lorenzo held her. Her limbs became leaden as all the blood to fuel them leaked from her throat. Her eyelids drooped slowly as she was pushed toward final slumber.

CHAPTER THIRTY

Nora's green eyes grew wide and fearful, her precious blood spilling from the gaping wound at her neck. Endre witnessed this all in a frozen state of shock before red rage descended over his vision. The terror in his *Elskling's* eyes was all it took for his mind to defer to the training of his upbringing as a warrior. The Viking in him was unleashed.

With a powerful yank of each arm, he pulled the chains from the grips of his captors amid their surprised and alarmed cries. They were merely background noise to the slowing thud of Nora's heartbeat filling his ears.

Blood continued to cascade from her throat, her mouth agape with unheard screams of agony. She struggled against Lorenzo's hold, her arms unable to perform the body's instinctual command to stanch the flow.

The Vampire within Endre struggled to keep his gaze from the red tide and growing pool at her feet. Although the blood called to him, the promise of enacting revenge on Lorenzo was a siren song infinitely louder than his desire to feed.

A deft flick of each wrist swung the iron links into wide arcs, catching his guards unaware when the metal separated skin and bone, leaving their heads separate from the bodies. More of Lorenzo's henchmen entered the fray from the shadowed corners of the chamber, no doubt stationed as sentries for an anticipated eventuality such as this. Lorenzo may have guessed Endre would put up a fight, but there was no way he could have foreseen the berserker unleashed the moment his blade touched Nora.

Endre's chains rendered guard after guard to pieces, like a warm knife through butter. Each downed guard brought him closer to the dais where Lorenzo stood, still clutching Nora while he watched the melee, a smug smile plastered on his face.

Slower and slower Nora's heart beat, and though he knew she would transition, it was not the way Endre would have chosen for her first death. The trauma of such a violent end nearly always indicated a violent beginning to a Vampire's second life. Whether Lorenzo knew she would transition or not was irrelevant, his blade across Nora's throat was clearly a calculated and premeditated catalyst for the ensuing battle.

He wanted a fight.

This realization dimmed Endre's rage. This was exactly what Lorenzo had hoped for—the irrational wrath of the bereaved. An emotionally driven combatant with impaired judgement, rather than a cold calculating warrior trained for winning battles. Endre harbored no illusions that the deal Lorenzo presented had been anything other than a ruse—a concocted scheme to lure him into believing there was a chance they would emerge from this chamber alive, and when Endre refused, Lorenzo would manufacture a reason to make sure they did not. The red dissipated from the edges of his vision, replaced with focused clarity brought on by the return of rationality.

Lorenzo had grossly underestimated his probability of winning. Endre could see the moment the villain realized his miscalculation. The self-satisfied smile slid from Lorenzo's face, his expression morphing into an irritated frown, right about the time Endre's body count reached past the two dozen range. It was impossible to tell how many more guards there were, but Endre did not doubt there were scores of reinforcements waiting in the wings if Lorenzo needed them.

Though his nemesis had never been much of a fighter in all the centuries Endre knew him, what he had been was cunning and clever. There were, without a doubt, layers upon layers built into this plan, but Endre had neither the time nor the patience to unravel them.

"Enough," Lorenzo commanded, dropping Nora's now-lifeless body to the stone at his feet.

Endre decapitated one last guard before allowing his gaze to slide to her corpse, her heartbeats silent. He regretted that he could not have spared her the pain, but from the moment Lorenzo first drew blood, her death had been inevitable. No amount of Vampire blood could have saved her in time, not with how her body processed it, and that was assuming he could have reached her before she bled out. All there was to do now was to wait for the transition and hope he could kill Lorenzo before he stole away her second life.

"I didn't bring you here for a fight," Lorenzo implored, a false smile tugging at the corners of his mouth.

Endre's gaze dipped down to Nora's still form, smeared with her own blood. "You have an interesting way of showing it." The cold edge in his voice promised a deadly conclusion to this encounter.

Lorenzo's malicious gaze held Endre's as he lasciviously ran his tongue along the blade of his knife, collecting droplets of Nora's blood. Closing his eyes, he swallowed with a satisfied moan before directing another arrogant smirk at Endre. "I do have to admit, after hearing how protective you were of your pet, I simply had to have a taste."

Endre forced himself to pull deep breaths into his lungs, pushing away the urge to abandon all thought to action and lunge at Lorenzo with each exhale. He knew when he was being baited.

"My, my, my." Lorenzo clucked with a chuckle. "I see your time in solitary confinement has taught you a thing or two about self-control. Now, I find that interesting, since I heard you gorged yourself on humans, leaving a trail of bodies on your way here."

"This banter is tiresome," Endre announced, keeping his tone deliberately bored. Stooping, he drew a sword from the scabbard of the last guard he killed and took a few more steps to close the distance between them. "It is time to end this."

Lorenzo's crooked smile faded, his eyes narrowing dangerously. "I'd have gone for the gun." With one swift movement, he tossed the dagger to the floor and drew a gun from a holster, aiming the muzzle between Endre's eyes.

By the time the report of the shot echoed through the chamber, Endre had already ducked from its trajectory.

Squeezing off another shot, Lorenzo stepped over Nora's body, the frustration of missing his target evident in the murderous glint in his eyes and the deep scowl creasing his forehead.

Endre continued to duck and dodge each shot. Even having been buried for nearly a century, his body still remembered what to do in a perilous situation. Lorenzo had never trained as a warrior and had never seen a real battle, whereas Endre had fought many. Wielding a weapon was in his blood, just as cowering behind a wall of guards was in Lorenzo's.

"Don't bring a sword to a gun fight," Lorenzo called out triumphantly with a jovial laugh when a bullet grazed Endre's cheek.

"You can save your banter," Endre growled back, ignoring the stinging wound. Ducking around a pillar, he calculated the likelihood of being able to pull a gun from one of the fallen guards around him before one of Lorenzo's shots hit their intended mark.

"I can see why you needed a guide to navigate the modern era, reaching for a blade instead of a gun. You always were so old-fashioned. I suppose that's what got you in this mess in the first place," Lorenzo taunted, his shuffling steps moving closer to Endre's cover. "It was always so hard for you to adjust to the times, to see how the world changed, and change with it."

"I imagine it will always be difficult for me to adjust to corruption," Endre answered, stooping toward the nearest fallen guard and peering around the edge of the pillar.

A gunshot cracked in the air, the offending bullet lodging itself into the stone a mere hairsbreadth from Endre's ear, sending him darting back to cover.

Lorenzo let out a laugh. "You won't last a month out there, then. This world is rife with venality. Perhaps it's best if I put you out of your misery." Stepping around the side of the pillar, mere feet away, he aimed the gun at Endre's forehead. "Goodbye to one final loose end," he announced, squeezing the trigger.

CHAPTER THIRTY-ONE

It was a sickening feeling, watching the blood pour from her body. Nora had nearly died scores of times since first crossing paths with Endre, but this was the *real* thing.

What was worse than the dying was the feeling of coming back to life—but only after what seemed like an eternity of limbo. Neither alive or dead, just *there.* Her eyes were frozen open, staring up at the stone ceiling, but her mind was still awake.

Then, suddenly, everything changed.

Nora could *feel* the cut across her throat closing up and her heart beginning to pump blood through her again—what little of it was left. Her eyes began to change. Everything around her was bright, as if she were outside in the daytime, instead of in this dank chamber underground, lit only by torches. The worst, though, were the fangs forcing their way through her jaw bone, pushing her shorter, human canines right from their sockets. Blinding pain radiated from her jaw, but her frozen body didn't so much as allow her a groan of agony. The transformation was nearly complete, in the end, she would cease to be her human self and begin her existence as a monster.

Today was both her death and her birth.

Gunshots sounded all around her, but her muscles wouldn't move properly when she tried to turn her head to look. There was shouting too, the words muffled at first, then loud. Too loud. It was as if she was suddenly pulled from the depths of a deep pool after nearly drowning. Air filled her lungs with a deep gasp, the light pierced her eyes, then faded slowly to something more manageable.

When strength returned to her limbs, she pulled herself to sitting and assessed the changes to her body as well as the overwhelming emotions and sensations which came along with them. Every sense was sharper, more focused. She could even taste the air around her—and right now, she tasted blood. Her blood.

Staring down at her red-stained hands, she ignored the din around her and tried to feel some emotion. Any emotion. She searched for the fear she felt when she saw her blood pouring from her body, but it was absent. What she found instead was unchecked anger and a hunger extending beyond her new reliance on blood to sustain her life. A craving for violence and vengeance overwhelmed all else.

Voices echoed off the walls, drawing her attention to the quarrel between her killers. They were both here, and she wanted a piece of each of them. Though Lorenzo had issued the final blow, if not for Endre, she never would have died, and she most definitely wouldn't have become this monster.

With more grace than she ever possessed as a human, Nora rose to standing. Every nerve ending along her skin buzzed to life as the air moved around her, each whisper a coded message about her surroundings. This would take some getting used to, for sure.

On silent feet, she crept toward the gunfight, cocking her head to the side to take in every rustling sound of Lorenzo and Endre's movements. The glint of metal in the torchlight caught her eye while a smile drew up the corners of her mouth when she retrieved her murder weapon from the floor. It would be perfect poetic justice to enact revenge with the very blade which took her life.

"Perhaps it's best if I put you out of your misery," Lorenzo announced, stepping with his back to her to point a gun at Endre.

Surprise coursed through Nora immediately following a wave of apprehension at seeing Endre cornered washed over her. This was unexpected.

Confusion replaced surprise and she shook her head in an attempt to put her emotions back into place. Concern for Endre's survival warred with her desire for revenge. No, it wasn't concern. It was something stronger, but she couldn't quite put her finger on it, as if her Vampire brain couldn't identify feelings outside the need for bloodshed.

"Goodbye to one final loose end," Lorenzo gloated, pulling the trigger.

Nora found herself mere steps behind Lorenzo when the gun clicked, his ammunition clip empty.

In a flash of metal, a deep growl sounded from within Lorenzo's chest as he dropped the gun and drew a sword from a sheath at his side, just barely blocking a blow from Endre.

A feral smile lit Endre's face as he squared off with his nemesis on a more evenly tilted playing field. "Swords do not run out of bullets," Endre cajoled as he reared back and struck again.

Lorenzo dodged the blow, stumbling a step backward and nearly running into Nora.

Endre's eyes locked with hers, his expression relieved. With a roar, he swung at Lorenzo again, the steel of his blade biting into his opponent's shoulder, cutting him to the bone.

A pained cry came from Lorenzo.

Endre glanced up at Nora again, a smirk pulling up one corner of his mouth.

Winged creatures took flight in her belly, the sensation bringing a gasp to her lips. Ah, now she remembered this one—it was attraction. She was wholly turned on by the sight of Endre swinging a sword. The visage of him as a warrior suited him, a homage to the blood memories of him laying waste to enemies on the battlefield. This was who he was at heart. The sight was utterly entrancing, and for the first time, she felt as though she was seeing the real Endre.

Indecision warred within her. Handsome though he may be, he was still half the reason she was a Vampire.

The smirk slipped from Endre's face, his eyes dropping to where Lorenzo's blade sliced through his abdomen, breaking the spell of his bright blue gaze and releasing her from the trance.

"I think you'll find you won't win this battle so easily, old friend," Lorenzo warned in a low voice. "I've had nearly a century of training in swordplay. It must be difficult for you, spending ninety years in the dark, dreaming of this moment, only to fail." Lunging with his blade, he aimed for Endre's neck.

Nora still held to the background, uncertainty plaguing her. It would be so easy to plunge the dagger in her hand through Lorenzo's back, stopping his heart. But what of Endre? How much blame could she place on him? Were his reasons for feeding her Vampire blood, knowing the risk of her transitioning, benevolent enough to negate her right to vengeance? Then there was the question of if she could even kill him? Weakness from her initial blood loss still plagued her and of course, she'd never wielded a weapon in all her life. But if Lorenzo killed Endre first, perhaps she'd fare better against him?

Lorenzo's blade missed its intended mark, but still managed to slice deep into the back of Endre's knee, dropping him to the stone floor. In a quick succession of slashes, he cut along Endre's arms and wrists, weakening his hold on his sword.

Endre knelt on the floor, his sword slipping from his grip as severed tendons rendered his hands incapable of gripping. His eyes flicked to Nora lurking in the shadows behind Lorenzo.

Once again, Nora found herself ensnared by his gaze.

Endre's expression remained impassive, though his eyes held a hint of sorrow. "Get on with it then," he ground out, his attention back on his executioner.

A hard lump formed in Nora's throat. This wasn't right. She couldn't let him die. Her new status as a Vampire may be half his fault, but he'd promised to make it right, hadn't he?

"I half-expected you to beg for your life, but I should have known better. You Norsemen with your belief of a divine afterlife in Valhalla. For your sake, I hope it truly exists." Lorenzo raised his blade for the final blow.

Blood dripped down Nora's hand when she plunged the dagger into Lorenzo's back and through his heart. The warm liquid oozed between her fingers, slickening the handle, and making it nearly impossible to grip.

Lorenzo let loose an agonizing scream, still very much alive.

Clearly, she misestimated on the location of his heart.

His hands scrabbled for the handle of the weapon, pulling it from his body with a gasp as he turned to his assailant. Rage contorted his features when he caught sight of Nora. Raising his blade, he lunged for her with a fearsome war cry.

Obviously, she hadn't thought this through—she no longer had a weapon to defend herself.

Before he reached her, his body was pulled backward, the sword clattering to the ground abruptly. Endre stood behind him, one hand gripping his hair, the other holding a sword poised at his neck, ready to end him.

"Wait!" Lorenzo rasped.

Endre didn't wait. Slowly, he slid the blade along the sensitive skin of Lorenzo's neck.

"I have your...ack. Your cure," Lorenzo choked out, his hands grappling with where Endre still held him.

A furrow formed between Endre's brows, his sword hesitating above his enemy's exposed throat. "You are lying," he accused. "If you had the cure, you would have led with that earlier." Pressure returned to the blade at Lorenzo's throat.

"You're right," Lorenzo wheezed. "I don't have the cure *yet*, but there's a lab. I have a team working on it, I swear on my life."

Nora searched the dark pits of Lorenzo's eyes for a lie, unable to decipher if his words held any truth.

"Your life means nothing to me," Endre spat. "You can take your falsehoods to your grave."

"Wait," Nora whispered.

"No, Nora," Endre protested, though he halted his movements. "It is all lies, he would say anything to save his skin."

"Where is this lab?" she interrogated, scooping the dagger from the floor and holding it loosely at her side, should she need to find a more effective way to threaten Lorenzo.

"Release me and give your word I walk away unharmed, and the lab is yours," Lorenzo choked out, even as Endre pulled harder on his hair.

"Let him go," Nora ordered warily, calculating how she could ensure Lorenzo was good on his word, and how to track him down if he wasn't.

Endre let out an exasperated sigh, but didn't relinquish his hold.

"If you let him kill me, you'll never find it on your own," Lorenzo warned, his eyes taking on a hint of manic glee.

"*Elskling*," Endre implored, "He speaks nothing but lies. We do not need his lab, we can build one of our own."

Lorenzo let out a hearty laugh, but Endre pressed the blade harder into his skin, cutting off any words he might have said.

Nora surveyed her murderer for a moment. What reason did she have to trust him? Red liquid dripped from the shallow wound at his neck, stalling all thoughts of labs and cures. Her eyes followed a droplet as it trailed a rivulet down the pale skin of Lorenzo's throat.

"Free me, and you'll have your cure. Occupy your mind with more important things than blood," Lorenzo whispered, his tone tinged in fear.

"I want to kill him," she answered, her gaze still glued to Lorenzo's blood.

"I think not, pet," Endre replied with a deep chuckle. "I have waited nearly a century to send this cretin to Hel. I will have my revenge." To punctuate his demand, he dug the blade deeper into Lorenzo's neck.

"He stole my life," Nora growled, her eyes heavy as they lifted to meet Endre's. "I want to watch the life dim from his eyes as I drain him of blood."

"You would throw away the chance I am giving you to regain a human life, for *revenge*?" Lorenzo pled.

"I will find our cure," Endre assured, his eyes still locked with hers, his expression resolute.

"You trust him? Look where that's gotten you? Dead. A Vampire," Lorenzo rasped frantically as his window of opportunity slowly swung closed.

Endre lowered the sword from his captive's neck, but kept hold of his hair.

Lorenzo heaved out a relieved breath.

"Continue to drink, even after his body goes slack," Endre directed, his eyes flicking down to the blood on Lorenzo's neck. "Just because he is unconscious, does not mean he is dead."

"No! Wait!" Lorenzo protested.

Running her tongue along her fangs, Nora ignored his pleas, her attention focused solely on the thud of his heartbeat and the glistening crimson on his skin. She closed her eyes and sank her fangs into the soft tissue of his neck, a primal part of her brain rejoicing in the act. Shouts and curses sounded from her victim and she caught a few choice words such as 'abomination' and 'mistake' along with plenty more ramblings about the existence of a lab and its lucrative business.

Each swallow was a welcome relief to the bone-deep burning which had accompanied her since awakening as a Vampire. Once the immediate need for blood was quenched, she began to notice the taste. Lorenzo's blood tasted different from Endre's, somehow oiler and almost putrid. As if the vileness of his deeds truly polluted to the very marrow of his bones, poisoning his blood.

Lorenzo moaned beneath her, his struggle less and less spirited. When the flow slowed and she felt like she was sucking pudding through a straw, she unlatched from Lorenzo's neck, not caring that she looked wanton with a new kind of lust, blood coating her teeth and dripping down her chin. She felt positively licentious. She smiled up at Endre and saw a spark of desire flash in his eyes before he gripped her arm and dragged her away from Lorenzo's corpse.

When she had stumbled a few feet away, Endre returned to the body splayed on the stone. He sliced his blade through the air and unceremoniously separated Lorenzo's head from his body, carrying out the death sentence to finality and fulfilling his vow to end Lorenzo's life.

They'd done it together, each getting their own version of vengeance from the wretched Vampire who was now in pieces at their feet.

Endre stalked toward her, and without slowing his pace, he threw down his sword at her feet and took her face in both hands. His lips met hers with bruising intensity, his tongue swiping out to taste the remnants of Lorenzo's blood still clinging to her. "I love you," he whispered into her lips, closing his eyes and pressing his forehead to hers.

"I don't feel a thing for you," Nora whispered back, plunging Lorenzo's short blade into Endre's side.

Endre chuckled as he looked down at the blade protruding from his body. Wincing, his hands wrapped around hers at the hilt and pulled at the blade.

Nora held the blade in place, watching his face contort in pain. It wouldn't be enough to pay back all he'd taken from her, but it would do.

"Looks like you feel plenty," he observed with a grunt.

"That's for dragging me into this mess," Nora growled. "So is this," she said, biting into the soft tissue where his shoulder and neck met, moaning in ecstasy as Endre's blood slid down her throat. She had been right; Endre's taste was decidedly different from Lorenzo's. Endre's was almost sweet, where Lorenzo's was rank with decay. Nora didn't know if she could stop herself. She thought draining Lorenzo might have sated this new, all-consuming need for blood, but it seemed it almost made it worse.

Endre gasped as she continued to draw his blood. "Now do you see?" he croaked out painfully. "You see what the blood does to you, how it changes, how it takes over your every thought? Now you see why I have to find a cure."

Nora tried to ignore the truth spilling from his lips. She *did* know; the blood was all she could think about now. She felt as though she would spontaneously combust if she didn't continue to consume the life of others. It was a debilitating need, taking away all reason.

"Nora, if you kill me, you will not survive. Hunters will seek you out. They will take away this second chance," Endre warned, his voice tight with pain, and yet he didn't struggle or try to push her away.

Why didn't he fight her?

As if reading her mind, he answered her unspoken question, "I love you. I will not fight you if you desire to take my life. I deserve it after all I have put you through. But if you wish to find a cure, you have to stop."

Now she understood the darkness he grappled with every day of his existence—it would be her battle now, too. The need to consume more and more blood drove every thought, and every instinct. To think of anything else would be a triumph over the very nature of Vampirism. It took monumental effort to pull her fangs from his flesh and step away from the glistening blood smeared across his neck.

Endre slid the dagger from his side, allowing it to clatter to the stone, his eyes locked warily on hers. "The fight is hard, but you are strong," he wheezed, pressing his hand against the wound at his side with a grimace.

Blood covered nearly half his body and Nora had to take a step backward, she didn't trust the Vampire in her to not go for the kill.

Endre's eyes closed for a moment too long and his body swayed before toppling to the stone floor.

His heartbeat pounded a sluggish rhythm in Nora's ears while hers grew stronger and steadier. By taking his blood, she was trading his life for hers. This is how it would always be—feeding from others—choosing her life over theirs. Standing over the barely breathing Vampire, she stared into his glazed eyes. Her mind flashed to the blood memory of him towering over her in the Italian sunshine, debating whether to save or condemn her. The irony of the reversal of the scene was not lost on her. Endre's life was at her mercy; she could either choose to save him or let him perish.

It was powerful.

She was powerful.

A manic giggle threatened to bubble up from inside her when the classic Spiderman quote, '*with great power comes great responsibility*' came to mind. Nora supposed being a Vampire was kind of like being a superhero, if done right. If done the way Endre did it—by punishing human scum by feeding from them, rather than the relatively innocent. One could easily slip the way of Lorenzo, taking on more of a super villain title if they weren't diligent—the two sides of a razorblade.

Nora cut across her wrist with her new fangs, the pain searing and abrupt. Crouching to the floor, she fed her blood to Endre, just as he'd done to her countless times, just as he'd done on that fateful day they'd first crossed paths. Endre sucked greedily from the wound in her flesh, and she had to hold him with her uninjured hand to keep him lying down when she finally pulled her arm away.

Taking in great, gasping breaths, his eyes went from glassy to alert. "*Elskling,* I am glad to see you decided not to dispatch me after all," he rasped with a wry smile.

"I decided I'd rather be a superhero than a supervillain," she told him with a shrug and smile.

Endre grinned back.

"And, I don't know the first thing about hematology and making Vampire cures," she said honestly, offering her hand to help him up.

"Ah, so you decided you needed me after all?" he questioned dourly, taking her hand. "I suppose I have to rely on more than charm and good looks to win your admiration."

Letting out a chuckle, she turned away, back toward the stairway they'd come down. Endre's grip on her hand stopped her from walking that direction, and a slight yank pulled her back toward him.

"Thank you," he offered somberly when they faced one another again. "You could have let me die. I

understand the difficulty in the choice you made."
Taking a step closer, he closed the gap between them.

Nora's gaze jumped from eye to eye, her breath hitching, and her heart racing when she anticipated what was coming.

Endre ran his fingers tenderly over her cheek, his hand snaking around the nape of her neck to pull her face nearer to his.

When their lips met, a sigh escaped her. Despite her best judgement, she was actually starting to feel something for him beyond lust. She wouldn't go so far as to call it anything anywhere *near* love. But the butterflies definitely indicated something closer to fondness than the complete disregard for his life which would have allowed her to watch him suffer through death. Not that she could admit that out loud to him, no need to inflate his ego. Regardless of her feelings, she believed in his ability to create a cure, and not only would that endeavor benefit her, but all those other Vampires out there who didn't want to be Vampires.

"You have saved me in more ways than you truly know. I am grateful for that and I will prove to you I am worth saving," Endre iterated, touching his forehead to hers and closing his eyes.

Surprised, Nora found herself nodding and swallowing past a lump in her throat while holding tears at bay. If not for the emotion and sincerity in his voice, she almost could have passed his comments off as sarcasm. But there was something so raw and vulnerable in the way he admitted her part in pulling him from the darkness enveloping him when he first emerged from his tomb, the words couldn't have been anything but truthful.

"Let's get the hell out of here," Nora choked out, clearing her throat to tamp down her tears, her emotions threatening to overwhelm the cold logic she needed to develop a game plan.

"Agreed," Endre said with a nod of acknowledgement.

Without a backward glance at the horror of the chamber painted with blood and littered with bodies, Nora led the way up the stairs. When they emerged from the building, the rising sun greeted her on the first day of her second life.

IRREDEEMABLE

BOOK TWO

With only the dying declaration of his enemy hinting at its existence, Endre and Nora set out in search of a lab to continue work on a cure for Vampirism. Having no direction to travel, they must venture to the lair of the enemy for clues, risking their second lives for the answer.

As a newly created Vampire, Nora must come to grips with the monster lurking just below the surface, begging to be unleashed and wreak havoc. Endre serves as a guide through the darkest moments, leading her to consider her feelings toward him may be more than simple lust.

The need to restore Nora's humanity and earn both her love and forgiveness drives Endre to drastic measures, which unravel the carefully building trust between them. Will a cure for the burdens of the second life he bestowed upon her be enough to redeem him for his barbaric actions?

AUTHOR'S NOTE

If you enjoyed reading *Irresistible*, please consider leaving a review wherever you purchase your books! I'd love to hear what you think of *Irresistible*.

Please consider signing up for my newsletter through my website at www.TaraVasserAuthor.com to get updates on new releases, excerpts from my works in progress, and offers for FREE books!

TARA LIVES IN THE FROZEN NORTH IN MINNESOTA WITH HER WONDERFUL HUSBAND AND TWO RAMBUNCTIOUS LITTLE DUDES. SHE IS AN ENGINEER DURING THE DAY, A CRAZY MOM IN THE AFTERNOON AND A WRITER AT NIGHT. SHE ENJOYS SPENDING HER TIME PLAYING IN THE DIRT WHEN HER GARDENS AREN'T COVERED IN SNOW AND LISTENING TO A WIDE VARIETY OF MUSIC THAT INSPIRES HER WRITING — SOMETIMES DOING BOTH AT THE SAME TIME.

Tara Vasser

Contact Tara

- Email -
TaraVasser.Author@gmail.com

- Facebook –
www.facebook.com/TaraVasserAuthor

- Website –
http://www.AuthorTaraVasser.com

- Twitter -
www.twitter.com/TaraVasser

- Goodreads -
www.goodreads.com/author/show/153
25170.Tara_Vasser

OTHER BOOKS BY TARA

Paranormal Romance

The Bloodlust Chronicles

Irresistible – Book 1
Irredeemable – Book 2
Irreplaceable – Book 3
Irrecoverable – Book 4
Irrepressible – Book 5
Irreversible – Book 6
Irrevocable – Book 7

Red

Red – Complete Trilogy

Contemporary Romance

Naughty Novella Series

Naughty Librarian
Naughty Professor
Naughty Nanny
Naughty Neighbor
Naughty Mechanic

www.ingramcontent.com/pod-product-compliance
Lightning Source LLC
Chambersburg PA
CBHW030423180626
46812CB00005B/2147